A Baby with my Billionaire Surfer

Summer West

Copyright © 2023 By Summer West

All rights reserved.

No portion of this book may be reproduced, distributed, or transmitted in any form or by any electronic or mechanical means, including information storage and retrieval systems, photocopying, recording, or otherwise without written permission from the author, except for the use of brief quotations in a book review and certain other noncommercial use permitted by copyright law.

This is a work of fiction. Any names, characters, places, or incidents are products of the author's imagination and are used fictiously. Any resemblance to actual persons and things living or dead, present, past or future, locales, or events is entirely coincidental.

A Baby with my Billionaire Surfer

Cover Designed by: Getcovers

Editors: Jo Gentry, Jeri Phelps

PB

Contents

1. A Splash of Trouble … 1
2. On The Edge … 7
3. At the Party … 12
4. Lights of Fate … 17
5. Rise and Shine … 23
6. Tower #1 … 27
7. Don't Look Back … 30
8. Rescue Me … 33
9. Too Many People … 37
10. Catch a Break … 41
11. The Gang's All Here … 46
12. The Storm is Brewing … 51
13. Another Storm on the Horizon … 55
14. Sheltered … 59
15. Lost Control … 66

16.	The Long Road	71
17.	The Puppet	77
18.	Splish Splash	82
19.	The Morning After	87
20.	The Date	89
21.	The Garden	95
22.	Surfing Coming up Next	99
23.	Ready to Go	104
24.	Fighting for Breath	109
25.	An Awakening	115
26.	Two Peas in a Pod	120
27.	On Love's Lost Shores	125
28.	No Knight in Sight	131
29.	California Dreaming	137
30.	Unwritten Invitations	142
31.	The Bridal Shop	149
32.	Rediscovery	153
33.	Soul Searching	159
34.	Two Days	163
35.	The Plea	169
36.	Trust In the Night	175

37.	The Last Gamble	182
38.	EPILOGUE	189

1

A Splash of Trouble

RYAN

"Watch out!" It's the only warning I can give before crashing into her.

"Ryan!" Violet exclaims, toppling off her surfboard into the California waves.

"Aw, hell." The saltwater slaps against my face as I unleash my board and kick through the churn to reach her.

"Sorry about that, Violet." She's coming up, sputtering, and I can't stop the chuckle escaping my lips. "Didn't see you there."

"Really?" she spits out, wiping the water from her face. "I'm on a bright pink surfboard, in a bright pink and black wetsuit, Ryan. How could you not see me?"

"I guess I was...distracted."

"Distracted?"

"Yeah, you know, just... riding the wave." I shrug, and a spark of laughter bubbles in my chest. "Guess I'm not the lifeguard everyone thinks I am."

She shakes her head, a small smile tugging at her lips, and it hits me then. She's more than Alec's shy, socially naive little sister. She's Violet, with her bright pink surfboard and her soft smile. And I just knocked her into the Pacific.

"Need a hand with that?" I nod towards her surfboard.

"If you wouldn't mind." There's a hopeful look in her eyes, and I can't help but smile.

"Of course, Vi." I maneuver her board until she can easily grab it. We hang in comfortable silence, the rhythm of the ocean a familiar cadence beneath us.

I give Violet a cheeky grin, reaching out to steady her surfboard. "Let me help you get back on."

She looks at me skeptically, but after a moment's hesitation, she pushes the board over to me. I position it steadily on the surface of the water, looking back to give her a reassuring nod. "Ready?"

Violet chews on her lower lip, looking like she'd rather face a horde of spiders than mount her rogue surfboard again. But there's a stubborn set to her shoulders that I admire. She nods, her grip tightening around the edges of the surfboard.

She starts to hoist herself up, her movements unsteady in the bobbing water. I watch her, ready to lend a hand if she starts to topple, but she manages to balance herself.

Suddenly, a wave crashes into us. We're thrown off balance, and Violet is pitched off her board again. I manage to stay on my board, turning around to check on Violet. She resurfaces, her face flushed and her hair sticking out in all directions.

"Oh, you look like a wet rat," I tease, unable to suppress a laugh.

Her eyes narrow, but there's no real heat in her gaze. She splashes water at me, her lips curving into a grin. "Shut up, Ryan."

"Hey, I'm just stating the facts!" I protest, but I'm laughing too hard to sound convincing. I haven't had this much fun in a long time.

She tries to mount her surfboard again, her actions more determined this time. And this time, she manages to stay on even when a bigger wave lifts us. Her laughter rings out, infectious and carefree, and I find myself grinning along with her.

As a good swell is coming, we are on our stomachs waiting to stand to ride the wave in. But the strong wave breaks just before reaching us. It knocks us off balance once more.

This time, though, we end up in a tangle of limbs and surfboards. The wave pushes us all the way to the shoreline. Violet underneath me, her wide eyes meeting mine in surprise.

"Ryan..." she begins, but I can't hear the rest over the roar of the waves and the pounding of my heart in my ears.

Suddenly, she pushes at my chest, breaking the spell. "Get off me, Ryan!"

Scrambling up, I extend my hand to help her up. That's when I hear it.

"Ryan? Violet?" Alec's voice cuts through the crashing of the waves, a note of confusion in his tone. We both look up to find Alec standing at the edge of the water, his surfboard under his arm. His gaze moves from me to his sister.

I help Violet to her feet, my heart pounding for a completely different reason now. I was never good at playing innocent. Especially when it comes to my best friend and his overly-protected sister.

I have a feeling Alec won't let this one go easily... and I can't say I blame him.

"Ryan! Violet!" Alec's voice rings out over the steady crash of the surf as we make our way toward him.

"What the hell are you guys doing?"

I shoot him a casual shrug, trying to downplay the awkwardness of the situation. "Just catching some waves, man."

Violet, on the other hand, doesn't seem too concerned about Alec's questioning. With a sly grin on her face, she flicks a glance at me before turning to her brother.

"Oh, you know, your best friend here decided it was a good idea to run me down with his surfboard. He almost drowned me, Alec."

I grin. Turning to face Alec, I notice his eyebrows climbing high up his forehead. His gaze ping-pongs between Violet and me, trying to gauge if she's joking. This is going to be fun.

"Oh, by the way, Alec," I change the subject before he can poke any more holes into the surfing incident. "I'm throwing a party at my place tomorrow night. You in?"

Alec grins widely at that, his eyes lighting up. "You mean at your estate, in your mansion?" he teases, laughing. Alec has always had a knack for making a spectacle out of my family's wealth. But he's never been envious or resentful. It's just another thing for us to laugh about.

"Yeah, that's the one," I respond, rolling my eyes at his theatrics. "Come on, it's not like you haven't seen it a million times before. And bring Violet along. The more, the merrier."

Alec turns to Violet, an inviting glint in his eyes. "What do you say, Sis? Up for a night of billionaire shenanigans?"

Violet stands with the sun highlighting the vibrant shades of her ginger curls. She rolls her eyes at us and shrugs, seemingly unimpressed. "Great, just what I need."

I give her a teasing smile. "Come on, Violet. What better way to spend a Saturday night than at the Ryder Estate? We have a chocolate fountain."

Alec bursts into laughter beside me. "He's not lying. The thing's absurdly tall. Like, you need a ladder to reach the top."

Violet raises an eyebrow at us. "Seriously? A chocolate fountain? Who does that?"

"I do that," I reply, puffing out my chest a bit. "And don't pretend you're not intrigued."

She snorts, flicking some water my way with a swift kick. "Oh, I'm totally captivated, can't you tell?"

"Watch it, or I won't let you near the chocolate," I warn her, though I can't stop the grin that spreads across my face.

"Sure, threaten me with that. I can live without your pretentious chocolate fountain," she retorts. But the mischief in her eyes gives her away.

"Anyway, I hope you guys will make it," I give them both a pointed look. "Wouldn't be the same without my favorite brother-sister duo."

Violet and Alec exchange glances. "Keep this between us, okay? Our parents..."

I nod. I know all about the Baileys and their traditional, reserved approach to life. My reputation as the neighborhood's playboy and surfer isn't their cup of tea.

"Your secret's safe with me." I wouldn't dream of ruffling the feathers of Mr. and Mrs. Bailey.

Alec chuckles. "Good, 'cause I'm not about to miss one of your legendary parties, even if it means sneaking out."

Violet groans, shaking her head. "You're impossible, both of you."

"Thanks! We try." Alec and I share a high five over Violet's protests. But I see excitement in her eyes.

"Alright, we better get going," Violet says, pulling Alec away. "We've got a party to prep for."

Alec, flashing me a wicked grin, allows himself to be led away. "Gotta get our beauty sleep, man. Your parties are no joke."

I wave them off, my mind already whirling with plans for tomorrow night. "See you guys tomorrow! And remember," I point a finger at them, "don't let the folks catch wind of this."

"Got it!" they chime in unison, their laughter fading into the distance.

Left alone on the beach, I grin at their retreating figures. The sun dips low in the sky, casting a golden glow over the shoreline. The waves lap against my feet, a rhythmic and soothing soundtrack to my thoughts.

I glance down at my phone, already buzzing with confirmations for tomorrow. But then, a new text notification catches my attention, the name on the screen causing my stomach to drop.

Dad

The message is short, concise, like always.

We need to talk. Now.

What could he possibly want to discuss? And why does it sound so urgent?

My mind races with possibilities, none of them good. The grin fades from my face as I pocket my phone and head home. The prospect of tomorrow's party is momentarily forgotten.

Trouble is brewing, and I can't help but wonder... What now?

2

On The Edge

VIOLET

As I watch my reflection in the mirror, my mind drifts to yesterday afternoon on the beach. Ryan Ryder, the notorious heartthrob. Me pinned beneath his chiseled body, a sea of shock and amusement dancing in his eyes.

His tanned, toned body against mine, the heat radiating from his skin, and the soft sand beneath us. I blush even thinking about it, and the giddy smile refuses to leave my face.

Heat floods my cheeks as I imagine his lips trailing down my neck, his hands sliding down to...

"Violet!" Alec's voice disrupts my thoughts, pulling me out of my imagination. I immediately jerk back to reality.

I blush harder, thankful that Alec can't see my face right now. "Y-Yeah?"

"Are you ready yet? You've been in there for an eternity," Alec calls from down the hall.

"Ryan's party isn't until tonight, you know!"

I roll my eyes, fighting back a smile. Oh, if only Alec knew. The last thing I need is my brother teasing me about my daydreams.

Especially when they involve a certain hunky lifeguard...

I text my best friend Alissa about the encounter with Ryan at the beach yesterday.

> *If you tell anyone that I daydream about Ryan,*
> *I swear I will wring your neck.*
> *Especially Alec. I mean it too!*
>
> Who me?
> I'd never tell anyone what a crush you have
> on the lifeguard known as Ryan.
> My lips are sealed.

Yeah, right. Like I'd believe that for a second. But she's my best friend and I trust her not to humiliate me in front of a crowd.

Still giggly from my Ryan daydream, I hop in the shower. We leave in an hour.

I choose a blue dress that hugs my every curve. Simple but making a statement. It's the perfect camouflage for a beach party.

Especially since we've told our folks we're off to a movie with friends. Friends who need to drop off a document at the Ryders on the way home. Our backup story if we get busted for partying at Ryan's.

Alec is anxious again. "Time's up Vi. We'll be late for the movie." His voice emphasizes 'movie' in case parents are listening.

"Coming!" I call back at Alec.

Giving my long, wavy ginger hair a last-minute fluff, I take in my reflection. My favorite silver pendant, a gift from Mom, lays against my chest, a tiny beacon of courage.

I breathe deeply, reminding myself I'm not that little girl anymore. I'm almost thirty...well I will be in two or three years...or four. I make my own decisions, even if it means bending the truth a little for a night of fun.

Stepping out into the summer evening, Alec's silver sports car sits in the driveway. It's an older model, but pristine, ready to take us to the weekend party.

Alec is obsessed with taking care of his prized possession. As I slide into the grey leather seats, the car hums to life, the scent of almost-new leather filling the air.

My phone buzzes in my pocket, the screen lighting up with Alissa's name. My best friend.

> Off to see your handsome Ryan?

Her teasing tone practically leaps off the screen. I text back, rolling my eyes, yet I feel the blush creeping up my cheeks.

> **Shut it, Lissa!**

> I heard Ryan got his tan on
> for the party. Going to be
> hard to resist that golden god.

My cheeks flare up at Lissa's words. She knows just how to push my buttons.

> **You're incorrigible!**

A grin spreads across my face. I can almost hear her laugh echoing through the phone. She texts right back.

> Just remember, Vi.
> Denial isn't just a river in Egypt.

I huff a laugh, shaking my head at her relentless teasing. Ryan and I are friends. Just friends. Denial or not, something tells me it's going to be a night to remember…I hope.

As we pull into the circular drive of the estate, a valet asks if we'll be staying long. If we're only staying for a short time, we can leave the car on the drive.

But we'll be staying all evening, so the valet takes our car. This estate is so sprawling that parking is more like a public lot than a home. A full staff is always on hand to accommodate guests. The Ryders are legendary for a variety of spectacular parties and social events.

There's no way guests would want to walk from the lot. Even the valets have golf carts to take them back and forth. Rolls Royce golf carts, of course. Money is no object.

The music is already booming as we step out of the car. We make our way to the back terrace near the pool where the party is in progress. A sea of people weaves around the pool, the terrace, the second-floor portico.

The crowd continues inside to the open ballroom of the Ryder mansion. Laughter and conversation melt into the night. Drink carts and bartenders are stationed throughout. Refreshments of any kind are never far from the guests.

I'm swept up in the wave of festivities, glancing around for familiar faces.

Then there she is – Alissa Ingram. A radiant smile on her face, a beacon in the crowd. Her eyes light up when she spots me. She weaves her way toward me, arms wide open.

"Violet!" She greets, pulling me into a warm hug. "You made it!"

There's an effortless grace to Alissa, her long dark hair falling in waves over her shoulders. Her tall frame and long legs carry her like a supermodel. Her complexion, a rich caramel, glows under the party lights.

Standing next to her, I can't help but feel a pang of envy. With my shorter stature, curvy figure, and pale skin, I'm like a vanilla scoop beside a caramel sundae.

Yet, as she pulls away from our hug, her eyes sparkle with genuine warmth for me. We're different, but best friends.

"Look at you!" Alissa beams at me. "You're so beautiful!"

"Shut it, Lissa," I retort, rolling my eyes playfully. "You're the one turning heads here."

As we step onto the party deck, loud music and chattering voices fill the air. A few brave, or maybe just drunk, souls are stripping down for a dip in the luxurious heated pool. Some are socializing in the massive sunken hot tub. If socializing means groping each other, then yeah, they're socializing.

My eyes drift across the crowd, seeking one particular face. Then I spot him. Ryan. Tall, muscular, with that beach blonde hair that always looks effortlessly styled. He's in the kitchen, drink in hand, and there's someone with him. It takes a moment for the realization to hit me.

Gemma. His ex.

3

AT THE PARTY

VIOLET

Why is she here? And why on earth is he talking to her?

"Do you need a drink?" Alissa asks, eyes scanning the room.

"No," I reply instantly. "You know I don't drink."

She rolls her eyes, a teasing smile playing on her lips. "No exceptions, huh? Even if it's the beginning of summer break? We're celebrating the end of our first school year of teaching!"

"You already know my answer, Lissa," I confirm, trying to keep my tone light.

"I'll go grab one for myself then. I'll be right back."

"No, don't leave me here!" My plea earns a soft chuckle from her.

"Relax, I'll be back in two minutes. I'll even bring you a soft drink." And with that, she slips away, leaving me standing alone, eyes still glued on Ryan and Gemma.

Alissa and I graduated from UCLA together. We both majored in education, so we became close when we had many classes together. She teaches 1st grade, me Kindergarten.

We took our time getting our degree. Alissa is a party girl, so we didn't take the traditional 4-year route. We stretched out our classes to take five years and one semester instead. Lissa frequently needed recoup time after all those parties.

We took a year after graduation to decide where we would land. Finally, we both received offers from an elementary school in nearby Torrance.

We both agreed we didn't want to teach in Malibu. Most of our students would likely be the children of our Malibu friends. We share a townhouse in Torrance but returned to Malibu for the summer.

I move to one of the big loungers by the pool, trying to squelch my thoughts. Then, as if on cue, the infamous Cole struts my way. My parents practically strong-armed me into a friendship with him. All because of some business relationship with his parents.

He's arrogant and repulsive, but I don't have much choice but to be civil to him. He plops down next to me, uninvited. "Having fun, Vi?"

Oh, I was having fun. Before you decided to ruin it. I bet he waited for Alissa to leave me alone just to swoop in.

"Mhm," I reply, keeping my eyes firmly away from his direction.

"Do your parents know you're here?" Cole asks, a smirk spreading across his face.

I fake a smile and am about to retort when I spot Ryan and Alec making their way toward us. My heart skips a beat. I'd never been happier to see them.

They both have a steely look in their eyes as they stare at Cole, as though they're about to strangle him. And for a fleeting moment, I wish they would.

"Catch you later," Cole grunts, standing up abruptly and walking away. Ryan, his arms crossed, maintains a hard glare as Cole retreats.

He then turns to me, the steely look softening. "A laser light show is about to start. We're gonna play a game. Come inside with us?" His smile is an invitation, but he and Alec are moving me along before I can reply.

"No, I really don't want--" Before I can finish my sentence, they're dragging me inside. Circles of light in multiple colors are swirling from the high ceiling.

Elliott, the life and voice of the party, grabs a microphone. The music quiets and the lights continue to bounce over the heads of the crowd. "Alright, friends, let's move this party up a notch. When I click this remote, the music will stop, and two green spotlights will stop on two lucky people. Those two will join together in a ten second kiss until the music starts again. Circle up under the lights and let's get started!"

This is ridiculous. I never played kissing games in middle school. What am I doing here now?

As I'm mulling over the game's absurdity, I glance at Alec, my brother. I'm surprised he's comfortable with me being involved in this. A shudder runs down my spine. Here's to hoping the laser never points my way.

But Alec stumbles off, laughing for no apparent reason. I guess that's just what alcohol does to him. His merry mood is infectious, though, and I find myself chuckling along, shaking my head.

I glance around for Alissa, but instead, my eyes land on Gemma. She's in the crowd clearly ready to play, inching her way closer to Ryan. Great, just what this game needs - Ryan's ex. I suppress a groan, wishing for a speedy end to this game. *Or a speedy escape for me.*

Gemma is striking. There's no denying it. Her wide, blue eyes captivate everyone around her. Her long, light brown hair flows around her like a waterfall. With her tan skin and perfect skin and body, she looks ready for the red carpet.

But, as beautiful as she is, there's a darkness beneath the surface. She cheated on Ryan, with multiple guys, no less. Yet here she is. Ryan, usually so smart and strong, was chatting with her earlier. Why would he even invite her? It doesn't make sense.

Pushing these confusing thoughts aside, I focus on the game at hand. A circle is forming, a mishmash of many of our friends from college. And apparently all in different stages of inebriation. The party lights cast an array of colors on everyone, creating a surreal ambiance as the music blares.

Laughter and chatter fill the air. The nervous anticipation for the game hangs over us like a thick, unbreakable tension. And right at the heart of it all, there's me, sober and feeling a bit out of place. But I'm here now, and there's no backing out.

Elliott holds the remote in the air and clicks so that green lights circle wildly around the crowd. Everyone's eyes are fastened on the lights, as if it were the most interesting thing in the world. The room falls quiet, the tension building. Then the music stops, and two green lights shine on two party goers.

Phew. That was close. The first laser points at Susan, the cute brunette from Zuma Beach. I think she went to Pepperdine. The second points to a guy I don't recognize.

The two 'lucky ones' meet in the middle of the circle. There's a moment of hesitation, and then they lean in, their lips meeting in a kiss that lasts a heartbeat. The crowd boos and jeers then chants, "10 seconds, 10 seconds..."

The two look at each other with a deer-in-the-headlights expression. Then Susan shrugs her shoulders and plants one on the guy. The crowd provides the countdown. And they make it! The whole 10 seconds.

Cheers, whistles, claps and laughter fill the air, and the party is alive again. The game continues as the green lights choose random pairs from the circle.

Dim lighting makes all the faces blur into one another as I watch, my heart pounding with a sense of dread. It's irrational, I know, but I can't shake off the anxiety creeping in on me.

Through the crowd, I catch sight of Gemma again. Her gaze is fixed on Ryan, her eyes shining with something I can't quite place. It's not admiration, it's not love. It's...something else.

Something that makes my blood run cold. Anger bubbles up inside me, so fierce and sudden that I almost gasp. But I swallow it down, trying to keep my face neutral. The game must go on.

"Come on, Elliott, toss me the remote!" Cole's voice slices through the noise of the crowd. I look at him standing directly across from me, where he has pushed his way into the circle, a smirk etched on his face. His words trigger a cheer from the crowd, as he catches the remote tossed from the stage. All eyes are eagerly watching.

As Cole points and clicks, I close my eyes.

Then, as if in slow motion, the green light shines on me. *Please don't let it be Cole!*

I open my eyes. And there, under the second green light stands a smiling Ryan.

4

LIGHTS OF FATE

RYAN

The spotlight stops...on Violet...And ME! She and I lock eyes for a fleeting moment, an unspoken conversation lingering in the air. A calculating grin starts to grow across my face. Then the silence is ripped apart by a familiar, grating voice.

"No way," Gemma protests, a fake pout on her face. The crowd mumbles and grumbles in confusion. Damn, I wish I hadn't seen her tonight.

The thing is, I didn't invite Gemma. That's my dad's doing. He's still hung up on the idea that Gemma and I are perfect together. That's what he texted me about yesterday. A little surprise in the form of Gemma's arrival. I hate how she's been flitting around me all night, and now, she's disrupting the game.

Without waiting for a response, Gemma grabs the remote from Cole. Her painted nails twinkle under the lights. A murmur of disbelief rises from the crowd as she clicks.

The lights swirl and whirl. The crowd falls silent, waiting, suspended in time, everything on hold.

Until the two lights again fall on me and Violet.

A wave of laughter breaks out from the crowd, their amusement as clear as day. My eyes dart back to Gemma, her pretty face contorting in disbelief.

"Seriously?!" she exclaims, her voice full of irritation. The crowd laughs harder. Even in the dim light, I can see her cheeks flushing, a sight that gives me an odd sense of satisfaction.

Then Violet snatches the remote and clicks again. The tension is even more intense this time as the lights circle the crowd. The laughter of the crowd is dying down.

And then, once again, as if the universe has a sick sense of humor, the lights stop... Pointing at Violet and me for the third time.

This time, I can't help but burst out laughing. The absurdity of it all has me doubled over, tears of mirth welling up in my eyes. The crowd starts chanting again, their laughter echoing around us.

There's no escaping now, the three spins have spoken.

"Kiss! Kiss! Kiss!" The crowd chants in unison, their cheers loud and insistent.

Her green eyes are wide, almost as if she's frozen in time. I don't give a damn about Gemma's protests now. I rise to my feet and walk over to Violet.

Her chest is heaving with each breath she takes. I take her hand to steady her. I lean in, and for a moment, we lock eyes. Her shock is apparent but there's something else, a spark of expectation, maybe?

With one hand cradling her neck, I pull her closer to me. My other hand finds its way to the side of her face, my thumb brushing her cheek softly.

And then I lean in, bridging the distance between us. The moment our lips touch, the crowd goes wild. There's a surge of energy around us, the crowd hollering and whistling in excitement. The crowd counts out the 10 seconds, but it feels like more. Yet, all I can focus on is the feel of her lips against mine.

We pull apart, the memory of our innocent kiss lingering. The crowd is still cheering, but the outburst from Gemma steals the spotlight. I can't help but laugh as she storms off, her temper flaring.

"Your girlfriend seems mad," Violet says, snapping me back to reality.

"She's not my girlfriend, Red," I reply, casually brushing off her words.

Red... It's fitting. Not just for her fiery hair, but also for her cheeks, flushed with embarrassment. Or maybe the excitement of our shared kiss. Whatever it is, she looks beautiful in the neon glow of the party lights.

"Know who else will be mad?" she challenges, raising an eyebrow at me.

"Who?" I play along.

"Alec," she states plainly. "When he finds out."

"He won't," I reply confidently, shrugging my shoulders.

She smirks. "Yeah, I bet he won't. They've already recorded it and posted it to their social media pages," her tone dripping with sarcasm.

"It's just a game, Vi," I reassure her.

I then shift my attention back to the noisy crowd. Grabbing the microphone and shouting over the music, "Hey everyone! As you all know, there's a surfing competition in six short weeks, mixed class, male vs. female this year! Plenty of time to practice and get your surf ready!"

The crowd responds with cheers and whistles, and the party atmosphere fills up the space.

"Everyone's invited!" I add, the excitement bubbling up in me. Confidence drips from my words as I boast, "Just know, I'll win. I am, after all, the best surfer in the area," I add in a taunting tone.

A wave of laughter and applause sweeps across the crowd. My eyes drift back to Violet, expecting to see a teasing smirk or a playful roll of the eyes. But instead, I see something else. There's a flicker of worry, a trace of anxiety in those green eyes, and I wonder... why?

I relinquish the microphone and move toward her. "You okay?" I ask Violet, noting the unease in her eyes.

"Yeah, I'm fine," she responds quickly, though the strain in her voice tells me otherwise. "I just... I assumed there would be a female class. I'm not ready to compete with all the surf bums around here."

I chuckle at that, shooting her a teasing glance, "I mean, you're not that bad."

A soft punch lands on my chest and she retorts, "Very funny, Ryder." Her words carry the pretense of irritation, but her eyes, those tell me she's amused.

"You know, I can train you," I offer, trying to stifle the grin spreading across my face.

"Yeah, like yesterday? When you almost drowned me?" Violet fires back, a mock grimace playing on her lips.

Her comment sends me into a fit of laughter. "Oh, you looked hilarious though."

"You're a riot, Ryder." She snaps and turns to walk away.

"Hey." I grab her arm and try to appear sincere. "No drowning, I promise."

She squints at me suspiciously, then finally sighs. "Fine, but if I end up at the bottom of the ocean, I'll haunt you for the rest of your life."

Violet's cheeks are still flushed with a delicate shade of red, and I grin as I watch her walk away. The atmosphere of the party suddenly strikes me as too intense. The laughter and music echo loudly around me.

I need to check on Alec. My best friend is probably making best friends with a toilet bowl right now. I head back into the mansion to find him, and the massive space overwhelms me even though I've lived here all my life.

Twelve bedrooms, sixteen bathrooms. No doubt several of them are currently occupied by people I'd rather not disturb.

Okay, think, Ryan. If I were a plastered Alec, where would I go?

Deep in my thoughts, I weave through the crowd of partygoers. An all-too-familiar figure approaches me. Cole. I've never been particularly fond of him. But social niceties required an invitation to the party.

He looks riled up, his usually slicked-back hair a mess and the smell of alcohol coming off him in waves. The guy is a couple of inches shorter than me. But right now, he's puffing himself up like he's about to take on a heavyweight.

"What's up, Cole?" I question, keeping my tone casual.

"You're gonna stay the fuck away from Violet, you hear me?" he snarls.

Taken aback, I throw on my indifferent mask, "What the fuck are you talking about?"

"You better stay the hell away from Violet, you understand?" Cole's voice slurs with the weight of the drinks he's consumed, his eyes glassy and unfocused.

"What's it to you?" I respond, raising an eyebrow, my tone cool.

"She's going to be my wife!" he exclaims, the words sloppy in his drunken state.

I laugh, the sound repeating in the nearly empty hallway. "And who told you that? Because I can assure you, Violet didn't."

"Don't you dare speak her name," he seethes, stepping forward, invading my personal space.

"And what if I do?" I challenge, standing my ground.

That seems to push him over the edge. He throws a punch, but I react fast enough to grab his wrist, stopping him. "Cool it, man. You've had one too many."

Security has been watching him all night. Two bouncers finally decide it's time to step in. As they peel his grip off my shirt and pull him away, Cole goes ballistic.

"And I'm going to beat your ass in the surfing competition too, you cocky bastard. You just wait and see!" The guard tightens his grip and forcefully drags him away, with Cole flailing and cursing all the way out. Security will call a cab to keep him from driving.

Had he been sober, I might have given him a real taste of a fight, but he was just a drunken fool tonight. Still, his words and actions boil my blood. Who does he think he is?

5

Rise and Shine

VIOLET

Barely able to keep my eyes open, I grope blindly on the bedside table. I knock over my alarm clock, a water bottle, and some books in the process. The incessant ringing finally stops when I manage to find my phone and snatch it up from the floor. The glow of the screen lights the room in a soft blue.

Alissa

I bolt upright, the fog of sleep clearing instantly. *What could she possibly want at this hour? Has something happened?* My mind races with various scenarios as I swipe to answer the call.

"Alissa?" I ask, my voice still rough with sleep. "It's 5 in the morning, what's going on?"

"Oh, silly. It's almost 8:30. Are you still asleep?"

"Of course, I'm still asleep. Why aren't you?" I mutter groggily.

"It's going to be a beautiful day! The warmest of the season so far. Let's go to the beach. I know which tower Ryan's working today," Alissa taunts in a sing-song voice.

Well, yes, now you have my attention! Suddenly wide awake and alert, I consider the possibilities. "But Alissa, you know I can't be in the sun all day. I'll come home cooked as red as a lobster."

"Don't worry. I have sunscreen...and a sun umbrella. We can set up for the day right in front of Ryan's lifeguard tower. If we get too hot, we can always walk up to the café and cool off for a while. But we need to get going. The beach will be crazy packed on a Sunday, especially if it's going to be warm."

"Ugh," I groan with resistance. But Lissa has thought this through. Finding out where Ryan's working. Foreseeing my objections and resolving them in advance. I feel coerced, tricked, back against the wall. "Okay. I'm in. Can you pick me up in an hour?"

"Yes, I can pick you up, but in twenty minutes. Slip on your suit and put some clothes on over it. Don't fix your hair or put on makeup. Just brush your teeth. I'll be waiting at your front door."

I jump up and put on my suit and pull a t-shirt and shorts over it. I throw a couple of towels and a blanket in my bag. I forage through my messy bathroom, looking for my sunscreen. I use sunblock made for babies. That's about how sensitive—and white—my skin is. Sunglasses, visor, wallet. Ready!

I don't hear anything downstairs. Maybe everyone's still asleep. Or gone. Good! I don't have to justify where I'm going or why.

As I slip out the door, my friend pulls up in her BMW convertible sports car. It's a beautiful shade of deep blue that matches her eyes. It's brand new and this is my first ride in it.

Alissa comes from a very wealthy family, like most people in Malibu. But not stinking rich like the Ryders, who have more money than God and Fort Knox put together.

The Ingrams own vineyards in the Santa Monica Valley. Her great-grandfather started their first vineyard in the 1930s. And now the business has grown through the third generation.

When Alissa's brother takes over the operations in a few years, that will be the fourth generation. Alissa didn't want anything to do with vineyards. That's why she went to college to become a teacher.

But she now admits that eventually she'll be involved in the business with her brother, Masyn. But she says she still has a whole lot of partying to do before that happens.

As we drive toward the beach, I can't help but wonder why Lissa set this up. "So, how do you know what tower Ryan's in today?"

"Oh, I have my ways," she says with a smirky grin plastered across her face.

"Come on, Lissa. Spill it."

"Well, I just happened to be talking to this friend of mine who is an LA County lifeguard in Malibu. When I found that out, I asked him if he knows Ryan."

"Let me guess, yeah, he knows him. Right?"

"Vi, he not only knows Ryan, he's in the same tower with him today! Cha-Ching!"

Curious, I delve deeper into this saga. "So how did you happen to be talking to another lifeguard? Where's he from?"

"I don't know where he's from, but I met him at Ryan's party last night. His name is Bobby Velasquez. When I asked how he knows Ryan, he told me they're working together today. He invited me to come hang out at his tower, after I convinced him there was nothing between Ryan and me."

"So, I'm coming along as your wingman? You like this guy, don't you? It sounds like he likes you."

"Yep, at least I think so. I just met him last night, but it might be a thing. That's why I want to be there today…for both of us. Double dipping, you see. I'll tell Bobby that I'm helping you get closer to Ryan, and you can tell Ryan you're helping me get to know Bobby."

This sounds fishy. I'm suspicious of the story, so I need to know more. "And then what happens when they talk to each other about us? We'll be so busted."

Alissa looks a little caught off guard. The confusion on her face tells me she has not thought of that scenario.

"Well, if we're successful, we'll all laugh about it later."

I'm skeptical, so I object. "Liss, I do not want to get closer to Ryan. I want to drool from afar. And if we happen to cross paths and start a conversation, then okay.

"But I'm not throwing myself at him. He can have any girl on the beach. I'm just Alec's little sister. I'm sure he has no interest in me at all."

"Well, that's not what it looked like last night when he kissed you," she teases.

"That was just a game. Not romantic. He had to kiss me. It was his game at his party. How could he refuse? Plus, I think he wanted to get back at Gemma."

"Well, what about when Ryan stood up for you when Cole confronted him."

"What are you talking about?" I inquired, totally lost in this conversation.

"Yeah, didn't you know? Cole told Ryan to stay away from you because you're going to be his wife! Ryan laughed in his face. When Cole took a swing at him, the security staff escorted him off the property."

"I didn't hear anything about that! How do you know?"

"Because it's all over social media, right after the video of you two kissing!" Alissa starts to laugh uncontrollably.

"That's not funny. Take me back home. I don't want to see Ryan. Please take me home."

"Too late. We're here. Just play it cool. We'll get our spot on the beach and let them find us. We won't do anything to attract their attention. One of them will see us and come talk to us. You just wait and see."

A nervous churning in my stomach is telling me it's not going to be quite that smooth. I have a sudden sensation of unsettling dread.

6

TOWER #1

RYAN

Still a little hung over from the party last night, I drag myself up the ramp to my lifeguard tower. Five minutes early for an 8-hour shift. And I can barely open my eyes, even with sunglasses on. I think it's going to be a loooong day.

I wonder why Bobby's not here yet. He's always the early bird. Maybe he had more to drink last night than I thought.

As I busy myself opening the tower, sweeping the sand, hanging the rescue tubes, I reflect on last night. What a wild one. First kissing Violet, then the scene with Cole.

After that little episode, I picked up the pace with my drinking. Violet and Alec left, and I felt lost and alone. In my own mansion. With a hundred of my closest friends.

Alec and I are like brothers. Best friends for years. And I kissed his little sister in front of everyone. Maybe that's why he wanted to leave suddenly. Or maybe because he was puking his guts out from drinking too much.

I sure hope their parents didn't catch them coming in last night. Especially since Alec had so much to drink. Mr. and Mrs. Bailey are incredibly strict, even with their children who are now adults. They do not let either of them make any decisions for themselves. That should be a criminal offense.

I am more than a little freaked out at the kiss with Violet. She was right. That kiss infuriated Gemma. Maybe that's why I kissed her. Plus, I kinda had to since it was my party.

But Gemma was hot. Later she started coming toward me and I just held up my hand. "Stop. I do not want to talk to you. We are not together, and I can kiss whomever I please."

She stopped dead in her tracks and just glared at me. Buried deep was a hint of hurt, but all she could show was anger. She turned and stormed out of the house without another word, and I never saw her the rest of the night.

Maybe she got the message. Maybe she thought I'd come after her. Maybe she went for a walk on the beach and threw herself into the ocean.

But I can't get the kiss out of my mind. There was a sensation I can't explain. The softness of her supple lips. Her warm breath mixing with mine. The way her neck relaxed into my hand as I pulled her close. She felt so...comfortable.

I think she felt something too. I could see it in her eyes the moment our kiss ended. A longing for it to continue. Wanting more but not letting it show.

What was I thinking? That's Alec's little sister. Not so little anymore. Only two years younger than me. We're both adults. Why does it feel wrong, but yet...so right?

"Hey, Ryan. Great party last night. Thanks for inviting me." Bobby greets me as he climbs the ramp.

"Yeah, it turned out all right, I guess. I think most everyone had a good time."

"Hey what was up with that dude that was yelling at you in the hallway?"

"Who, Cole? Oh, that was crazy. You know that girl I kissed during the game? He told me to stay away from her because she's going to be his wife. And then he took a swing at me. If he hadn't been so drunk, I probably would've gone a round with him."

Bobby has a confused look. "Does the girl know she's gonna be his wife?" he chuckles.

"That's what I said. I'm quite sure she never agreed to that. He's kinda creepy."

Bobby always has all the latest from HQ. "Today's going to be the warmest day of the summer so far. Expecting a large crowd. We need to be on high alert. Double check batteries in the radios. Then check in with headquarters to verify our landline is working."

"Gotcha. I've done it all but call on the landline." Bobby nods his head and gives me the thumbs up as he goes inside and picks up the phone.

When he hangs up, he updates me. "They just told me no one leaves the tower for a break. They'll bring around food and let us take a break later. They are really preparing for a big crowd. The biggest so far this season. Plus, conditions are right for a rip current to cause problems."

I'm not worried. I try to reassure Bobby, who is in his first season as an ocean lifeguard. "No worries, my brother. We've got this under control. Plus, we always have immediate backup if something happens."

Bobby looks a little worried, but he knows I've got his back. I feel like I've been doing this all my life. I've been guarding this beach since I was 18 years old. And I was a junior lifeguard for two years before that. This is my 12th season at Malibu Beach. I've never wanted to go to another beach.

"We need to conserve energy this morning while it's not crowded yet. It could get stressful this afternoon if there's a big crowd."

Just then I see something out of the corner of my eye. Could it be? I think it is. *Violet.*

7

Don't Look Back

VIOLET

Alissa and I grab our things and hurry down to the sand. We walk along the back edge of the beach until we are behind Tower #1. Then we make our way toward the water until we are beside the tower.

"Is this spot, okay?" I ask Lissa.

"No, let's go a little closer to the water. Until we're in front of the tower, but off to the left. Not directly in front. That'll be too obvious. And remember -- Don't look at them. Just you and me. Setting up our little space in the sand for a day at the beach."

"Got it," I reply. "Don't worry. I'm not going to turn around and look back. Like you said. When they see us, they'll come talk to us if they can."

So, Lissa and I spread out the blanket. She sets up her beach umbrella, my safe zone if I need to get in the shade for a while. *Crap. I forgot to bring music.*

Alissa is unpacking her things. Oh good. She brought a cooler with some water and a couple of soft drinks. And my hero...she brought music!

We pull off our clothes and double check our swimsuits. We don't want to get thrown off the beach for indecent exposure.

Now we're set. Operation 'Don't Look Back.' The morning sun is still at our backs, so we start out lying on our stomachs facing the ocean.

"Doesn't this feel wonderful?" Alissa says with such serenity. It's like she was made for this. Relaxing. Feeling the warmth of the sunlight on her back. *Dammit. I didn't put on sunscreen.*

"Yes, it does feel wonderful, my dear friend. But it won't this afternoon if I don't get some sunblock on," I say as I anxiously dig through my bag. Ah-hah! Got it. "I am glad I remembered this. Usually, I don't remember to put it on until I'm already burning."

Alissa is so lucky. She never burns. She has that bronze glow all year round. Me? Sometimes I think I can get sunburned just looking out the window. And I NEVER get tan. Only varying shades of pink. Light pink, dark pink, bright pink, and finally RED!

Well, I can't put the lotion on my back, so I ask Alissa to help. "Gee, I wish your lifeguard Ryan was already down here to put this on for you," she smirks.

"Shut it, Liss. He's not *my* lifeguard. Have you seen *your* lifeguard Bobby yet?"

"Yes. I sneaked a peek while we were walking up this way. He had his eyes on the water and didn't notice us."

"Good. I have a bad feeling about this little plan of yours."

"My plan? I believe it was OUR plan."

"Not really. I just agreed to come along."

Alissa looks hurt. "Are you sorry you came?"

"No, of course not. I'm just afraid I'll get all glassy-eyed if Ryan does see us and come down to talk."

"Don't stress, Vi. Ryan's a smooth talker. He won't make you feel uncomfortable."

"Well, they probably won't come down here anyway. But Bobby might. He sounds intrigued by your effervescent personality."

Then we hear it. "Will the two ladies with the beach umbrella please come to the lifeguard tower? Please come to tower #1."

It's Ryan's voice. Alissa and I snap our heads to look at each other. What the fuck? "Well, I guess they saw us," Alissa deduces. "Come on. Let's go."

8

RESCUE ME

RYAN

"Hey, Bobby. Look down there by that pink and yellow beach umbrella. Does that look like Violet?"

"Who's Violet?"

"You know, the girl I kissed during that game at the party last night."

Bobby takes a closer look through the binoculars. "Red head with alabaster skin? Yeah. That's her. And she's with that girl I was talking to last night. Lisa, er Lissa..."

"Alissa. She and Violet are best friends. Watch this."

I grab the bullhorn and buzz it. "Will the two ladies with the beach umbrella please come to the lifeguard tower? Please come to tower #1."

Both of us laugh as we see them snap their heads and look at each other. "Why'd you do that?" Bobby asks.

"Because we can't go down there. And they obviously came here to our tower for a reason. But I wonder how they knew where I'd be."

Bobby ducks his head. "That would be me. When Alissa and I were talking I mentioned you and I were working together today at Tower #1. I told her to stop by and hang today. I didn't know she'd bring a friend. Sorry."

"No, don't be sorry. I'm happy to see them. I love to get Violet flustered and watch her face turn all shades of pink and red. She's always been extremely shy. Her parents have raised her under a rock.

"Last night was the first time she'd been to one of our parties since she was in high school. And she had to lie to her parents to come with her brother. Here they come."

I walk about halfway down the ramp to greet them. "Good morning, ladies. How are you today?"

"Very funny Ryan. Why'd you call us over here? Just to embarrass me?" Violet snarls.

"Hello, Miss Violet. I'm glad to see you too. Where's Alec? Still in bed?"

Violet laughs at me. "I have no idea. I didn't see anyone when I left this morning. I don't even know if he came home last night. Alissa took me home from the party and I told Alec to find a ride."

I reassure her. "Yeah. I had my driver take him home. He had no business driving as much as he'd had to drink. We'll get his car back to him this afternoon when I get off work."

I turn my attention to Alissa. She's slyly taking glances up at Bobby, who's still watching the water. There's not a big crowd yet, so Bobby's taking his fair share of glances down at Alissa too.

"Good morning, Alissa. Did you have a good time last night?"

"Of course. There's never any doubt about a party at Ryder Estate. Always the place to be." She smiles ear to ear as she continues her gaze up at Bobby.

I lean down closer to her and whisper, "Do you and Bobby have a thing going?"

Alissa snaps out of her mesmerized gaze at Bobby. "No. Why do you think that? Did he tell you something?"

I chuckle at her probing question. "No. But I'm a very astute and observant lifeguard."

"Oh, Ryan," she whines. "You're always trying to stir up something."

"Who me?" I respond, feigning innocence.

Bobby yells sharply to me. "Ryan, two o'clock."

My eyes turn immediately to my right, looking out into the surf. Yep. There are two girls floundering and waving their arms. "Good catch, Probie. Call it in then follow me."

I grab the rescue tube hanging on the tower and race down the ramp. "Be back in a few, ladies. Don't go away."

VIOLET

Alissa and I stand frozen in time as we watch Ryan dart across the sand. "Excuse me, coming through," he repeats, warning the beach bathers to stay out of his way.

As he reaches the water's edge, he runs through the shallow water lifting his knees high. Once a little deeper, he dives under each wave and continues until he gets to the struggling swimmers.

By the time he reaches them, the girl with blonde hair has disappeared beneath the surface. I see Ryan push his rescue tube in front of the dark-haired girl just before she goes under.

He makes sure she is holding on tight to the tube. Then he dives deep under water, searching for the submerged victim. He's under water for what seems like an eternity, then resurfaces. He looks around, semi-panicked, then dives under the surface again.

Alissa and I look at each other, still unable to speak or move. Witnessing this emergency is turning our relaxing beach day into a frightful ordeal.

Bobby arrives with another rescue tube and attends to the remaining swimmer. Just then, Ryan surfaces with the unconscious blonde. Bobby helps get her leveled out so Ryan can tow her in.

Sirens are blaring. The rescue vehicle drives through the crowd to assist. As Ryan reaches shallow water, the newly arrived rescuers take the blonde-haired victim.

Bobby is right behind, pulling in the dark-haired girl. She seems shaken but not in dire need of medical attention. He assists her to shore and takes her to the rescue truck where she is checked out by a lifeguard from another tower.

Meanwhile, Ryan and the rescue team work on the blonde. They perform CPR, trying to bring her back to consciousness. A crowd gathers to watch, as a junior lifeguard tries to keep them back.

Suddenly, the crowd erupts with cheers and applause. We realize they have successfully revived her. Next, they place her on a backboard. After loading her in the back of the emergency vehicle, they zoom away with both girls. A dramatic demonstration of skill and efficiency.

Alissa and I both take a breath. I feel like we have been watching in slow motion. Consumed with concern, worrying not just about the swimmers, but Ryan and Bobby as well. I never imagined how worrisome it is to watch a friend risk his life for a stranger.

After the girls are taken off to the emergency room, Bobby and Ryan make their way slowly back to the tower. Lissa and I are waiting for them, and we both give them hugs of congratulations for an amazing rescue. Both guys are still breathing heavy from the exertion of their call to duty.

They are followed by an official looking lifeguard carrying a clipboard and a radio. Ryan tells Bobby, "Here comes all our paperwork. Just focus on the details of the rescue for the report."

Alissa quickly interjects, "We'll head up to the café to get a bite to eat so we don't distract you. I'll text you to see if you want us to order something for you."

Both the guys just nod and give us an aimless flip of the hand. We know they hear us but are deep in concentration.

9

TOO MANY PEOPLE

VIOLET

Alissa and I make our way up the hill to the Cena Bocadillo. I think it means something like Snack Bar. At least that would make sense, because...it's a snack bar.

The uphill climb is challenging and by the time we make it inside, we are both famished. After looking over our lunch choices, we both settle on a spinach salad. It's topped with strawberries, candied pecans, and grilled chicken. And finally, veiled with a raspberry vinaigrette.

Our food comes quickly as we chat about the rescue we witnessed. We are proud of Ryan and Bobby. It was nice to see them in action.

So many people think lifeguards are just people to give you directions. Plus pick up trash while watching people work on their tans. But lifeguards have a real purpose. And Ryan and Bobby just showed everyone on Malibu Beach the real purpose of lifeguards.

"So, when we get back, are you going to talk to Ryan?" Alissa inquires.

"What about? The rescue?"

"No silly. Well, yes, if you want. But don't you really want to talk to him about being your surfing coach?" she suggested.

I'm dumbfounded. "Why would I want to talk about that? He was just kidding when he said that last night. He probably doesn't even remember he offered."

"Hmm. Well, I'm going to talk to Bobby. If I think he's into me, I may ask him out. Do you want to ask Ryan and we'll go on a double date?"

"NO!!! I'm not dating Ryan. He's my brother's best friend. We are totally just friends." I try to shut down her overzealous idea. "But I think it's a great idea for you to ask Bobby out. He seems really nice. You two might just hit it off. Who knows?"

Lissa thinks about that for a second. "Why do you fantasize about Ryan all the time if you don't want to date him?"

"I can't help it. Visions of him float into my thoughts, and I can't help but feel the electricity of his touch, even if it's only in my mind. But *no one* can know about that, right Miss Ingram?"

"Whatever you say, Miss Bailey." We call each other by our teacher names, a signal that we're totally serious.

"Well, you better text Ryan and see what they want us to bring them."

"Me? You're the one who offered."

Alissa gives me her smirk and takes out her phone to send Ryan a text. He replies right back, and she shows me his response:

> **No, but thanks Lissa. We have food from HQ. But you're coming back to the beach, aren't you?**
> **I want to talk to Violet.**

I can't believe it. I wonder what he wants to talk about. "Tell him yes, we're coming back right now." And off we go back down to the beach.

VIOLET

We're surprised so many people have arrived at the beach in the short time we were gone. There are too many people for Ryan to come down to talk to me, but he waves for me to come up in the tower.

I try to contain myself. I resist the urge to go running up the ramp. Lissa and I fake an intense conversation, not looking at the guys in the tower. Then I hear his voice.

"Violet, come up here for a second." I force a surprised look.

My heart is racing as I walk slowly up the ramp, trying to control my breathing so I can speak. "Hey, Ryan. What's up?" I wait for his reply.

He talks to me without taking his eyes off the water and the people he's protecting. "You wanna surf in the morning? I have an executive board meeting at Ryder Enterprises at 11:00, so I can only go for a couple of hours. I can pick you up at 6. You in?"

I swallow my breath, so I don't sound too surprised or eager. "I guess I can. I didn't think you were serious last night. Do you really want to coach me for the surf competition?"

He turns his head quickly towards me. "Of course, Violet. I wouldn't have offered if I didn't mean it. I wouldn't leave you hanging like that. It'll be fun." His gaze returns to surveying the water.

"Okay then. I'll be ready at 6:00. Pull around to the garage door. That's where my board is."

"Sure thing. Wear your heavy wetsuit. The water's cold at 6 in the morning."

I smile as I agree and turn to go down to our beach blanket. Alissa is sitting there, watching every move and every expression during our conversation. "Okay. You didn't have to stare at us the whole time we were talking."

"How else am I going to advise you of Ryan's intentions? He looks at you like…I don't know how to describe it. But it's not like his best friend's little sister. That's for sure."

"Shut it Liss. We've already had this conversation. We're just friends."

"Whatever you say, Miss Bailey." And we both laugh as we start to pack up our belongings.

"Aren't you going to go talk to Bobby?"

"He looks busy. The beach has gotten a lot more crowded while we were at lunch. I'll catch him some other time."

"Really?" I blurt. "You pushed and prodded me to talk to Ryan and now you're chickening out? That's weak, Liss."

"Okay. I'll run up there for a quick second, just to tell him good-bye and see if he wants to get a drink after his shift."

She runs up the ramp and I can see Bobby's eyes light up when he sees Alissa is there to talk to him. I can tell he's agreeing to what Alissa is asking. Now she's putting his number in her phone and returning to our spot.

"There now, don't you feel better about that?" I ask. "Let's pack up and get out of here. There are way too many people here now."

10

CATCH A BREAK

VIOLET

5:30 a.m. I haven't slept a wink all night. Every time I close my eyes, I see Ryan and me in various compromising situations. Not that I don't want any of them to happen, but I can't let myself think that way right now.

My only focus is on being a better surfer for the competition.

5:50 a.m. I'm standing outside my garage with my surfboard ready to go. I'm wearing my warmest wetsuit. I have towels and a comb for my hair. I can't think of anything else I'll need. We won't be there very long.

Ryan has an executive board meeting at 11:00 so we'll need to leave by 9:30. I won't need a snack, but I better grab a bottle of water. I turn to go back in the garage when Ryan pulls up in his dark red Toyota pickup truck. It's a custom design he special ordered.

Extra-long bed and a special built-in locker to keep his surfboards secure. No need to tie them on the roof. Just slide them in the back and lock the cabinet door. The cabinet will hold four boards and another two can be strapped to the top of the cabinet. Whoever said money can't buy everything, definitely did not know the Ryders.

After Ryan slides my surfboard into the cabinet, he walks around to open my door. Not being chivalrous, but to help me with the step up into the big ass truck.

"So Vi, how are you getting away with going surfing with me? I'm sure your parents wouldn't be okay with this."

"Fortunately, when Alissa brought me home from the beach yesterday, she came in with me. We told my parents she was taking me surfing this morning, so no more questions. Why do you ask?"

"I just wondered if Alec knows and is covering for you or what."

"Nope. Alec doesn't know," I respond as Ryan gets a very smug grin on his face. "Okay, what's the grin for Ryder?"

"Oh nothing. Alec looked a little disapproving last Friday when he found us surfing together. Just wondered if he knew about today."

"I think I told him about you offering to help me, but he blew it off like it was a joke. Where are we going, anyway?"

Ryan answers, "I thought we'd try Tequila Bay. Have you ever surfed there?"

"I've never heard of Tequila Bay. Where is it?"

"That's my little secret. Very private. It'll be a great place for your first lesson."

Hmm...first? Implying more than one?

The rest of the short drive is filled with loud music and no conversation. Very comfortable. No pressure to come up with something to talk about.

Once we arrive, Ryan pulls the truck over to the side of the road to park. "No parking lot? Are we allowed to park here?"

"That's right. It's a small out-of-the way bay. Not much traffic on this beach. We don't even have lifeguards at this tower anymore. It'll be the perfect place to work on some basics. So you won't feel self-conscious."

Well, that's thoughtful of him. I guess. Is it so I'm more comfortable or so he won't be seen helping a rookie like me? Whichever, I think it is a good choice.

Ryan carries our boards down the bank and onto the sand. I follow with our towels and my bag. "Ryan, do you want to put your keys in my bag?"

"Nope. I attach my fob to the loop in the pocket of my board shorts. It's in a waterproof case so I can always keep it on me."

Ryan walks to the water's edge and lays both boards down in the sand, while I spread one of the towels to set down my bag. "Why are the boards in the sand?"

"Well, we are going to start our first lesson on land with the basics."

"Ryan, I've been surfing for a while now. I know the basics. Let's just get in the water."

"Patience you must have, my young Padawan. So much to learn you have."

"Thank you, Yoda. What's next? Fighting with light sabers? I just want to surf."

"Okay, Vi. Just trying to lighten you up a bit. You seem a little tense."

You think? A little? "No, Ryan. I'm fine. Let's get on with the sand training."

"Well, first, you need to learn how to lie on the board properly. Balance is everything, and it starts on your stomach."

Ryan lies on his board and motions for me to do the same. "You want the board to stay flat as much as possible, so you can't be too far back on the board. That makes the nose come up and you're screwed before you even catch a wave."

Ryan drones on and on about paddling out to the lineup. I think he's noticed that I'm not paying much attention. "Okay, Vi. Let's practice standing up once the wave is carrying you. So, show me how you usually do it."

After I make my feeble attempt at popping up, Ryan tries to be encouraging. "Okay. Not bad. We can work with that. First, when you pop up, stay down low. Standing up too quickly will take you out. Stay down until you know you have your balance. You try."

I'm on my stomach again and pop up, this time staying in a crouch position. Ryan stands behind me and grabs my hips as I pop up. This startles me so much that I stand straight up and turn to look at him.

"What are you doing, Ryan? You scared the bejeezus out of me. You might warn me next time."

Ryan just laughs like it's the most hysterical thing ever. "Sorry, Vi. I'm going to guide your hips to help you get in the correct position. That's why we're still on the beach. I can't correct your hip position once we're out in the water."

"Okay. I'm ready this time." I repeat the move again, this time ready for him to grab my hips from behind. But this scenario is too much like the visions that kept me awake last night. My heart races and my breath grows shorter and faster.

The anticipation makes my knees weak and when I pop up, my legs can't hold me, and I fall backward on top of Ryan. *Holy fuck shit!* "Oh, Ryan. I am so sorry." I cringe as I roll to get off him. "Are you okay?"

Ryan is literally rolling on the sand laughing at me. For a moment, I am offended, but then the humor washes over me, and I join him in a good hearty laugh rolling in the sand.

"Do you think we can try that again, Vi? I'll be ready for you this time."

After we both regain our composure and the air becomes serious again, I return to my stomach for another try. *Pop up, stay low, weight balanced. Got it!* This attempt is much better. He steadies me as I feel for my balance. But the sizzle from his hands on my hips is so distracting, I am barely balanced enough to stand.

"Very good. Much better."

"Well, I guess so. I didn't knock you down this time." His hands linger on my hips, and I wonder what I'm supposed to do now.

"Okay. Once you're on your feet, you keep your weight back." He pulls me back closer to him. I gasp for air again. I can feel the warmth of his chest on my back through my wetsuit. His breath on my neck gives me shivers.

"That's it. You're doing great. Keep pressing down with your back foot to keep the nose up above the water slightly. If the nose dips in the water, you'll fall face first. Trust me, it's not that fun."

"Okay. Let me try it again by myself." I need him to let go of me so I can catch my breath. And slow my heart that's beating out of my chest.

I make several more attempts, each better than the last. Ryan adjusts my hips a few times, but mostly stays back watching me.

"Well, coach. Are we ready to go out in the water and catch a break?" Ryan seems distracted.

"Yeah. In a minute. I think we may be getting company."

11

THE GANG'S ALL HERE

RYAN

Violet's a quick learner. She'll be in shape for the competition, for sure.

Oh no. This can't be! A group of guys is assembling on the top of the hill, and they don't look friendly. I don't want any trouble. Especially with Violet here.

El Manada. This gang thinks this is their private beach and no one else should surf here. I thought early on a Monday morning would not piss them off, but I may be wrong. There's only three of them right now. I'll make peace before the rest of the gang shows up.

"Stay here, Violet. I'll go check it out. No matter what, don't leave this spot. Got it?" I demand.

Violet looks scared. I shouldn't have been so forceful. But I don't want her following me and getting in the middle of some gang war. *It's not going to be a gang war, Ryan. Just talk peacefully with them and agree to leave if they want us to.*

I walk about halfway up the grassy hill. "Hey, guys. What's up?" I say with all my charm and innocence.

"Ryder, what you think you're doing on our beach with your hotsy-totsy down there? Can't you find another place to play grab ass?" Slate, the leader of the group, crudely demands.

Well, that fires me up. But I stay calm. *Calm and agreeable. That's the only way to avoid violence.*

"Hey, Slate. No worries. I'm giving surfing lessons now. That's my first student. She's not very good and very self-conscious, so I brought here where it's usually deserted."

The group grumbles at the idea of me bringing a stranger to their beach. "I honestly didn't think you'd be here this morning. Just let me finish this lesson, and we'll be out of your way."

"I don't think so, pretty boy. Pack it up and get outta here."

I'm ready to agree to leave peaceably. But then Granger, the first lieutenant, adds, "But you can leave your little cutie here. We'll teach her a thing or two for you." The other two laugh and urge him on.

That does it. That's too much for me to let slide. "You'll keep your hands off the lady. Mind your manners boys and we can all play in the sandbox together."

I slowly start backing down the hill, creating distance but not turning my back on them.

Granger yells, "Yeah…And who made you king of the sandbox. Let's get him, guys." He charges at me and the other two follow.

I was afraid of this. I tried to keep the peace, but sometimes you just can't. I hate fighting, but there are only three of them. I can't let them get to Violet.

Granger gets to me first, running straight at me with his arms wide, ready to get me in a head lock. He's easy. I just duck, grab his arm and kick his leg out from under him. He flips onto his back with a thud. He's just stunned. He'll be back up in a few seconds.

Now the third guy gets to me. I lean forward pushing my shoulder into his gut. He flips forward and rolls down the hill, landing face-first in the sand.

Now Slate. Probably the toughest of the group. I'm faster and taller, but he outweighs me by a hundred pounds. I'm also smarter. Just as we start to tangle, Granger grabs me from behind, pulling both my elbows behind my back.

He thinks he has me now, but he's actually given me more leverage. Using Granger for stability, I push Slate away with my left foot and give him a swift kick to the head with my right foot. Down goes Slate.

When Granger regains his balance, he throws his weight forward on me. I lean forward and quickly push my hips backward into his lower body. My momentum going downhill frees my arms. I grab Granger's head and pull him forward, over me and onto his back.

They each make another feeble attempt at knocking me out, but I am in much better condition, and they wear down fast. Regular required ocean swims of 1000 meters keep me in better shape than surfer gang bullies. For sure.

I turn to see the third guy with no name nearing Violet. *I told her to stay there. And why is she carrying her surfboard?*

―――ele―――

VIOLET

I stand in the sand, not moving from my spot as ordered by Sir Ryan Galahad. It looks like he's just talking to them, but they don't look so pleased. I can't hear what they're saying, but I hear their grumbling, grunting sounds. And it doesn't sound like "Welcome to our gang, Ryan."

What is he thinking? If I'm not mistaken, those guys are part of the El Manada surfing gang. They're a dangerous bunch and it behooves one not the cross them. I've heard about them all my life, but I've never come across them. That's one advantage of having parents that kept me under a rock most of my life.

Now Ryan is backing slowly down the hill. Retreating but not turning his back. He doesn't trust them to stay away. Then I hear, "Let's get him, guys," and the three charge at him.

Ryan is pretty good at Mixed Martial Arts, so maybe he can handle three gangbangers. *Is that what they're called? Gangbangers? I think so.* He flips the first one onto his back. Then the second is thrown down the hill and onto his face in the sand.

Now he's facing the big kahuna. *I don't know if that's the right term, but I need to help Ryan.*

I pick up my surfboard and slowly sneak my way across the sand. I don't know what I'll do with my board, but maybe I can pass it to Ryan to use as a weapon.

As I peek out from behind the board, I see one of the guys coming at me. *Why would he want to hurt me?* Not being a fighter, I have no idea what to do.

"Stay back, I'm warning you," I shout, trying to make myself sound as fierce as a 5'2" pale weakling can sound. He laughs and rushes toward me. I look at Ryan. He sees what's happening, but can he stop the guy before he gets to me?

Panicked, I put the surfboard on top of my head. I don't know why. Maybe to make me look bigger? *I don't know. I've never been in a fight before.*

I can tell he's getting closer. *Should I run back toward the water? I don't know what to do.* I decide to fight. I start to turn the board to put it under my arm just as the big guy is about to grab me.

I swing the board at him with all my 5'2" might and hit him in the head. *I can't believe I did that.* The guy falls into the sand and doesn't move. *I think I knocked him out.*

I look at Ryan and he is laughing as he runs toward me. When he reaches me, he grabs me up and spins me around, surfboard and all.

After he puts me down, I ask him sternly, "Why are you laughing? That was scary for me, Ryan. I didn't know what to do!"

"What were you thinking? I told you to stay back no matter what. But the sight of my little mighty mouse taking down one of the gang with her pink surfboard is a sight I'll not soon forget. That was so awesome...But you should've stayed back."

Just then, I see the two guys Ryan took down on the hill rushing at us. "Ryan," is all I can muster as I point at the oncoming trouble.

"Don't worry, Vi. I've got this." And he reaches into the pocket of his board shorts. Next thing I know, I hear sirens.

The two guys running at us stop and look at each other. Then they go get the guy I knocked out, get him up to his feet, and drag him off. And just like that, they're gone.

"Whew. I'm glad that's over. But how did you call the police? Do you have a Bat Phone in your pocket?"

12

THE STORM IS BREWING

RYAN

A Bat Phone in my pocket? Where does she come up with these things?

I can't help but burst out laughing at the Bat Phone comment. "No Vi, I don't have a Bat Phone. But I do have a button on my key fob that turns on a siren in my truck."

"What? How come?"

"I'll tell you over lunch. Are you hungry?"

"Well, maybe a little. But you have a board meeting."

"I'm bailing out today. The fight wore me out. Plus, I don't feel like explaining how I got a busted lip."

"You need to get some ice on that lip to keep the swelling down. Didn't I see a cooler in the back of your truck?"

I'm impressed. "Very good, Nurse Violet. I think I'll do that. Let's take our stuff up to the truck. After I get some ice, we can go get lunch. My treat!"

Violet agrees and grabs her stuff. I carry both boards up to the truck and lock them in the back.

"There's a little place just up the road. Cena Morada. Have you been there?"

"No, I don't believe I have."

"Well, it's nothing special, but they have really good food. I always eat there when I surf at Tequila Bay. The people are nice. I think you'll like it."

"Can we go in our wetsuits? I don't have any clothes."

"Ahh…fair point. I've always got something in the truck. What do you have on under your wetsuit?"

"Just a swimsuit."

"Perfect. I have an extra pair of shorts and you can wear one of my lifeguard zip-up jackets. It'll be a little big, but it's better than a bathing suit."

Violet agrees and we get in the truck and head to the little diner up the road. It only takes a few minutes to get there, and we hop out of the truck. Violet kind of slides out. It's a long way down for her.

As we enter the diner, I can tell it's not crowded. It rarely is. The place is so neat and orderly. We are greeted as soon as we come in the door.

"Hi, Ryan. It's good to see you today. Who's your friend?"

"Hi, Jorge. This is my friend, Violet. Violet, this is Jorge."

"Pleased to meet you, Miss Violet. Welcome. Please have a seat wherever you like."

"Let's sit over here by the window, Ryan. It's a beautiful view of the bay."

"Excellent choice," Jorge comments, then leads us to the table for two.

"Miss Violet, I believe violet is a shade of purple, isn't it?"

Violet answers Jorge, "Yes, it is. Just like the décor in here. Purple is my favorite color."

Jorge laughs. "Ah, that's great. Cena Morada means Purple Diner. Purple is my wife's favorite also."

Jorge gives us menus and says he'll be back shortly to get our order. Violet and I look at our menus and decide on the grouper sandwiches. Before we get a chance to order, the front door slams shut.

Startled at the sudden intrusion of the quiet, Violet and I both look toward the door.

Gemma. *What is she doing here?* She storms straight over to our table and demands to know what we're doing here.

"Uhhh...having lunch. What are *you* doing here?"

"I saw your truck and just wanted to pop in and say hello. But I had no idea you were here with *her*. What's going on Ryan? Why are you doing this to me?"

"Gemma, I think I made myself clear Saturday night. We are not together. Beyond that, what I do and who I do it with are none of your concern."

Gemma looks hurt, but I don't care. How does she think I felt when we *were* together, and I found out she was sleeping around? With three different guys! I will not relent. She means nothing to me.

"Ryan, please. Please don't do this to us. Especially with her, whoever she is. She's nobody. You and I are meant to be a power couple. We are destined to be together."

"Okay, Gemma. Now you've pushed me over the edge. We are NEVER going to be a power couple. Maybe we were on that path, but it ended when you decided to sleep with Tommy Gates."

"But Ryan, I told you how sorry I was. You said you forgave me."

"I did forgive you Gemma. And then you slept with that guy from the art museum. And then there was the movie producer. What did you think? I'd just keep forgiving and forgetting? Get out of here and leave me alone."

Now I can see the venom in her eyes; her begging and pleading has turned to poison. "Well, I don't think your father will approve of the way you're treating me. Especially when he finds out you're hanging out with the likes of her. Believe me, he won't be pleased."

"You judgmental little *bitch!* You cannot come storming in here like a hurricane and make threats. I will have lunch wherever, whenever, and with whomever I want. Stop following me around or I will get a restraining order. How will that affect your pristine public image? Don't push me, Gemma. It won't turn out well for you."

She turns around with a humpf and marches out the door. When I look at Violet, there are tears welling in her eyes. She tries to blink them back, but it's clear she's upset. Before I can try to settle her down, she bursts out with apologies.

"Stop, Violet. You did not do anything to be sorry for. We're just having lunch. We're just friends and Gemma Weston does not control my list of friends. I'm sorry she upset you."

I put my hand on top of hers, trying to comfort her. "Let's put it out of our minds and try to enjoy our lunch."

Jorge meekly makes his way to our table. "Is everything alright, Mr. Ryan?"

"Everything is fine, Jorge. I apologize for the intrusion. That was totally unacceptable behavior. I hope you can forgive me for raising my voice in your establishment."

"Ryan, you were provoked. You handled the situation quite well, in my opinion. No harm done. Now, what can I get you two for lunch?"

13

ANOTHER STORM ON THE HORIZON

VIOLET

"Wow. That was a lot to eat. I'm stuffed. But it was fabulous. I don't think I've ever had grouper that delicious. And so many fries. I think I'm ready for a nap now."

"Oh no, Violet. It's back to the beach for us. Time to get out in the surf and up on your board. You ready?"

"I need to walk it off or I'll throw up out on the waves. It's not too far, is it? Can we walk back to the beach?"

Ryan looks at me like I have two heads. "You wanna walk back to the beach carrying our boards? It's over half a mile. Can you walk that far?"

"Of course, I can. I walk over a mile almost every morning. Not carrying a surfboard, but I think I can do it. It'll be fun. It been a crazy day with the El Manada gang and Hurricane Gemma storming into our quiet lunch. Maybe a walk will bring everything back into perspective."

Ryan looks hesitant but agrees. "Okay, but I'm not carrying your board."

I just smile and stand to leave. Ryan stops. "Wait a minute. I need to go pay Jorge and thank him for our lunch."

"Yes. Please tell Jorge I thought everything was wonderful. And I love the purple décor."

Ryan laughs and walks back into the kitchen to talk to Jorge while I start to go out to the truck. But I stop myself before I go out the door. *I better wait for Ryan. What if Gemma's still out there stalking us? Or the El Manada is waiting for revenge?*

It is just a minute or two until Ryan reappears. "Were you waiting for me to open the door for you?" he says with an amorous grin.

"No silly. I wanted to wait for you in case there are any more surprises waiting out there for us."

"That's probably a good idea, given our day so far. Let's get our boards and head for the beach. Do you want to take your bag too?"

I reply quickly. "Of course. I need my hairbrush. My hair looks awful when I get out of the water."

Ryan gives a loud chuckle. "I remember. Like a wet rat."

"Shut it, Ryan. That's not funny."

He just rolls his eyes but doesn't say anything else.

So, on our stroll back to Tequila Bay beach, we talk about everything that's happened today. He tells me the story about the siren in his truck.

"Well, my truck is the same model and color as the LA County Lifeguard emergency trucks. So, I have a siren in case I need to respond to an emergency when I'm off duty.

"There are no flashing lights, but I have a single bubble light in the cab I can put on the roof if I need it. It's kind of like having an undercover lifeguard vehicle.

"A lot of fire fighters have them in their trucks. Since lifeguards are part of the LA Fire Department, it works out that I can have one too."

I am intrigued. "Well, it sure came in handy this morning. I hope I never see any of the El Manada gang *ever*."

We are walking along the shoreline, on our way back to our surfing spot. When we are almost to that section of beach, I notice the temperature has dropped. Looking out over the water, I can see dark clouds hovering. "Is it supposed to storm this afternoon, Ryan?"

"I don't think so. But I thought we'd be leaving at 9:30, so I really didn't pay attention to the forecast for this afternoon. I think we're okay. Those clouds are way out. They're not coming inland. But it may give us a little rougher surf."

Concerned, I ask, "Is that good or bad for my lesson?"

Another chuckle and Ryan replies, "Well, good for surfing. Jury's out on how it affects your lesson. Come on, let's go." And he takes off running to our spot.

"Hey, wait up. I never said anything about jogging." And I slow down to a walking pace. He'll just have to wait on me.

By the time I reach Ryan, the thunder is getting louder, and the clouds look darker and seem to be moving faster. "Ryan, are you sure we're going to be alright?"

"Relax, Violet. I'm a trained lifeguard," he flaunts with authority. "Would I let anything happen to my best friend's sister?"

Oh, thanks for reminding me, Ryan. I had almost forgotten. "Can't I just be Violet and not Alec's sister for a change?"

Ryan looks straight into my eyes with a seriousness that almost makes me nervous. "I'm sorry, Vi. I didn't realize that bothers you," he admits with sincerity. "From now on, you're Violet, my friend. And not Violet, Alec's sister."

I just smile back at him. "Thank you. That'll be nice."

Suddenly a clap of thunder stuns us. "I think that was close. Are you sure we're safe with lightning in the area?"

Ryan has a concern on his face that worries me. He's looking around the beach like he's trying to find something.

Then he admits, "Walking probably wasn't the best idea. And what were we thinking? We took our wetsuits off at the diner and didn't grab them from the truck. We couldn't surf now if it was sunshine and 80 degrees."

"Oh fuck, Ryan. What are we going to do?"

"Violet...I've never heard you say the 'F' word before. I'm appalled," he teases.

"Well, that is because you're always with Alec when you see me, and I don't say it in front of him."

Ryan just laughs at me. "I didn't know you have a different vocabulary when you're around Alec."

"Well, now you do. And now it's starting to rain."

Ryan surveys the sky. "Yep. I think we need to head back to the truck before it gets too bad."

As soon those words leave his lips, the skies open. I've never seen it rain so hard so suddenly.

"Run for the tower." Ryan yells as he takes off toward the lifeguard tower. It has been pushed to the back of the beach just below the grassy hill.

By the time we get to the tower, we are both soaked to the bone. We duck under the tower to escape the downpour. The thunder and lightning are increasing and it's getting cooler. Or maybe I'm just cold from being wet.

"Okay. We'll leave our boards down here under the tower. Push the nose down deep in the sand so the wind doesn't pick it up and blow it away. You stay here while I go up and see if I can get the door open."

Ryan rushes around and up the ramp. I can hear him rattling on the door. Grumbling and mumbling words I'm sure I don't want to hear. Then I hear a loud thud. "It's open Violet. Come on up. I had to kick it in, but it's open."

I run up the ramp, trying not to slip on the wet surface. Ryan's waiting for me and ushers me in, closing the door behind us as we are finally sheltered from the driving rain.

Once protected from the storm outside, we stand looking at each other. *What do we do now?* I wonder.

14

Sheltered

VIOLET

My heart pounds in my chest. There's a strange intensity to this moment, the storm raging outside. The sudden closeness inside this small room.

I take a deep breath, trying to compose myself. We're just friends, right? But then why is my heart beating like crazy? Why is everything suddenly so different, so intense?

"Are you okay?" Ryan's voice is close, too close. His worried gaze locks onto mine.

I muster a small nod, pushing a wet strand of hair away from my face. "Yeah, I'm fine."

Relief washes over his face and he lets out a small laugh. His comment catches me off guard, "You look funny when you're wet, like a wet rat." I gasp, feigning outrage as I punch him playfully in the chest.

"Will you stop calling me that. It's not funny anymore."

With a sigh, I sink down onto the floor, wrapping my arms around my knees. There's a sense of comfort sitting here, with the rain falling heavily outside. Ryan follows suit, plopping down beside me. His shoulder brushes mine, causing a ripple of warmth to spread through me.

Despite the chill of our drenched clothes, his presence brings an unexpected sense of coziness. We're shoulder to shoulder, knee to knee, and I find myself wondering if this is how friends normally feel.

A shiver courses through me, interrupting my thoughts. I wrap my arms tighter around my knees, attempting to generate some warmth. But the wet fabric of my clothes clings to my skin, making it all but impossible.

"What's in your bag, Vi?"

"Oh, yeah. I've got towels. They might not soak up very much as wet as we are, but they'll help some, I guess.

"Maybe we should take our wet clothes off," Ryan suggests. My head whips towards him, my gaze piercing into his. He lifts his hands defensively, "I'm not trying to be a pervert. I just... they're making us colder. Then we can dry off with your towels."

"Good thought." I proceed to take off Ryan's loaned clothing. "Here's your jacket and shorts back." I joke as I throw them at him. "And here's a dry towel. It might have a little sand in it, but better than nothing."

Ryan follows suit, removing his shirt, leaving us both in our swimwear. He dries off as much as he can.

After drying off, I slide back down to the floor, clutching my knees, my towel wrapped around my shoulders. The towel is so wet it doesn't provide much warmth, but it makes me feel covered, sitting here in nothing but a swimsuit.

Ryan sits down beside me deep in thought, plotting a solution no doubt.

Ryan notices my discomfort. He rummages through the sparse contents of the drawers in the lifeguard tower. "There is nothing in this tower, but I'm not surprised. It hasn't been used in over a year. But maybe...."

He spots a small cabinet on the back wall. He pulls on the handle, but it won't open. He reaches to his left under a built-in shelf and pulls out a key. "Ah ha!"

The key opens the cabinet that holds a first aid kit and a blanket, a flashlight and an old two-way radio but not much else.

"Here's a blanket for you. Dry off as much as you can with your towel then wrap this around your shoulders. That should warm you up a bit."

Then with a sigh, he slumps back down next to me, his brow still furrowed in concern.

His hand delves into his pocket, pulling out his key fob and his phone. "What are you doing?" I ask, watching him with curiosity.

"Looking for a signal," he replies, his voice tinted with a hint of frustration. The screen of his phone remains stubbornly void of any bars.

With a sense of dread, I pull my phone from my bag, praying for a miracle. But it's the same. No signal.

Ryan shakes his head. "We're too close to the hill. The signal is blocked from getting down to us. This is not a great area for cell service anyway."

"Can't your fancy key fob signal your truck to come get us?"

Ryan laughs, but then realizes I'm probably not kidding.

"Sorry, Red. It only has a quarter mile range. You're freezing," his concern etches deeper lines into his forehead.

"No, not freezing..." I try to brush it off, my teeth chattering slightly. "But cold, yes."

"I'm sorry," he says, shaking his head. "This is my fault."

"Hey, don't," I counter quickly, shaking my head too. "I'm the one who wanted to walk back from the diner, remember?"

"But I'm the one who said the storm wouldn't bother us. That was while we still had time to go back."

"So, if anyone's at fault, we both are." Despite the circumstances, I appreciate Ryan's concern. It's nice...comforting.

"I don't feel warmer," I confess through chattering teeth.

"Yeah, me neither," he admits.

Ryan peeks out the door to check on the storm. Still raging outside, the sky has grown darker. The lone lightbulb hanging from the ceiling is dead. We have little more than vague outlines in the dim light. I suppose it's a good thing - he can't see me clearly in this state.

As the minutes tick by, the chill seeping into our bones pushes us even closer together. Ryan puts his arm around my shoulder pulling me close trying to keep me warm.

I realize I'm hogging the blanket, so I put part of it around him. In an unspoken agreement, we end up huddled, trying to share what little warmth we can muster. His arm wraps around me, pulling the blanket tight around us both. I don't protest.

Instead, I nestle deeper, my senses filled with the scent of him – no artificial fragrance, just Ryan. It's unique and strangely soothing. I return the gesture by wrapping my arm around his waist. Snuggling my shoulder under his outstretched arm.

The stillness of our moment extends. We remain tangled, half-dressed, and seeking warmth in the other's body. Heat creeps up my cheeks. It's an embarrassing blush, realizing the intimate setting we've created for ourselves.

The word 'cuddling' flashes across my mind, and I feel my heart flutter at the thought. I try to suppress it but can't deny that my trembling has eased a little, replaced by a different sort of warmth. I feel safe. Sheltered.

"Are you warmer now?" Ryan's voice is low, a deep rumble that vibrates through his chest to mine. I glance upward to meet his gaze. I find his hair damp and tousled from the rain, his eyes looking down at me with concern.

"A-a little," I stutter, surprised at the shaky note in my voice. It's almost as if my body is reacting on its own accord, responding to his presence in a way that is new.

In response, he tugs me closer, his arm tight around me. His hand moves to my thigh, rubbing it gently in an attempt to generate warmth through friction. Yet, as his fingers create a pattern against my skin, it's not the cold that's my foremost concern anymore.

Instead, I'm hyperaware of his touch. The heat radiating from him. The fast rhythm of his heartbeat under my hand that's resting on his chest.

The real question now isn't whether I'm warming up. But what exactly is happening to my body in response to Ryan's closeness and his touch?

My mind spins as his hand roams higher up my thigh. His touch is electric, sending a current of heat up my spine. The way his fingers trace my skin is not just about generating warmth anymore, it's... intimate, sensual, almost arousing.

"R-Ryan..." I manage to stutter out, but my voice trails off, unsure of how to address what's happening.

"Yes?" His voice is low and husky, his breath warming the side of my neck. His hand pauses, but he doesn't pull away.

"I... uh..." Words abandon me, and I'm left stuttering, my heart pounding like a drum in my chest. His closeness is overwhelming, all-consuming. The boundaries of our friendship are blurring, and I'm not sure what's on the other side.

It's terrifying and thrilling at once. I swallow, attempting to regain my composure. But I'm far too aware of his hand on my thigh, of my breasts pressed against the side of his chest, of his warm breath on my neck.

Gently, Ryan leans closer, his lips hovering near my ear.

"Maybe...you could sit on my lap," The intimate proposal sends my heart into a frenzy, and it takes me a moment to process his words. A rush of warmth surges through me, definitely not from the blanket around us.

I shoot him a disbelieving glare, wondering if he's being serious. But the earnest look in his eyes confirms it. I hesitate, weighing my options. It's freezing, and his proposition is practically a lifeline.

"Fine," I mutter, my voice trembling just as much as the rest of me. "But no funny business, got it? This is just...to get warm."

He raises his hands in mock surrender, a small smile at the corner of his lips.

I take a deep breath to steady my nerves. With a slow caution, I shift to straddle his lap. His arms encircle my waist almost immediately, pulling me snugly against him. Our bodies align in a way that has my heart thudding erratically inside my chest.

The intimacy of our position is undeniable. His firm chest is pressed against mine and our crotches touching. The heat radiating from him envelopes me entirely. It's washing away the lingering coldness from my skin.

I become overly conscious of our bodies - particularly the way my crotch is pressing against his. Trying to ignore the sensation, I bury my face in the crook of his neck. I draw in the scent of the sea and sand clinging to his skin.

His hands, which were initially resting at my waist, start to move. A slow, almost hesitant journey that ends on the curve of my backside. My breath hitches as his palms come to rest there, heat searing through the thin fabric of my bikini.

I bite down on my lower lip, willing the silent gasp stuck in my throat to stay buried. The mere closeness to him is dizzying, intoxicating. It's the kind of heat that stings but is too enticing to pull away from.

His touch is both gentle and greedy, and with each passing second, I can feel my resolve crumbling. He pulls me closer, pressing me into him. His bare chest presses against my bikini-clad breasts. My center resting directly over his emerging hardness.

As his big, warm hands explore the curve of my butt, a gasp escapes my lips. He's not just touching me, he's holding me – possessively. His fingers slip under the edge of my bikini bottom, and I freeze, my breath hitching in my chest.

He gives a soft squeeze, eliciting a gasp from me. The sense of his hardness pulsates beneath me. It's far too provocative for my body to remain unaffected. I feel myself getting wet, my body responding in a way I never imagined.

I pull away slightly, meeting his gaze. His eyes, usually the color of the clear sea, are now dark and heavy with desire. His cheeks are slightly flushed, his lips parted as he looks back at me passionately.

"Is this okay?" he asks, his voice a rough whisper against the rhythm of the storm outside.

His question is a lifeline. A chance to halt this progression before we completely blur the lines of our friendship. But we are both too far gone to stop now.

I respond not with words but with a slow grind against him. My body moves intuitively, guided by a rhythm as old as time itself. A soft moan escapes my lips.

All the while, our eyes never break contact. His gaze is intense, almost predatory, drinking in my reactions as I move against him. His mouth parts slightly, a silent gasp, a copy of the surges of pleasure coursing through our bodies.

And I can feel him – feel his length – hard and demanding beneath me. Oh, he's...big. The realization sends a rush of heat pooling between my thighs. I should stop this. I know I should. But do I want to?

15

Lost Control

RYAN

Heat's crawling up my neck, pooling in my chest, as I feel her grind against me. I'm trying to hold back, dammit, but all the self-control in the world couldn't keep me from wanting her. And I can't stop my damn moaning either, as if I'm a hormone-fueled teenager all over again.

And hell, it's not just me. She's right there with me, gasping and clutching onto me like her life depends on it. The way she's grinding on my cock... It's driving me insane, pushing all my buttons. Shattering my restraint into a million pieces.

I groan, pulling her closer, moving faster, harder. I place my hands on her soft shoulders, my fingers slipping under her bathing suit straps. With a swift, sure move, I slide my hands under and down her arms. With a graceful, flowing move, she lifts her arms out of her straps. And then her suit is down to her waist.

With a surge of adrenaline, I grab her breasts, pressing my palms into their soft, yielding flesh. Whoa, they feel even better than I'd ever let myself imagine - smooth, warm, and perfect.

The electricity zings through me, straight to my already hard cock.

Her lips find mine, a fierce clash of passion and years of repressed desire. It's like the dam of self-control has finally broken, a wild current sweeping us away. The taste of her, the feel of her, driving me to the edge of insanity.

I slide my hands down her back and inside the bottom of her swimsuit. I feel the cheeks of her ass and squeeze them firmly. She lets out a small yelp of surprise. How adorable. How I want her.

She reaches for my shorts, her delicate hands struggling to yank them down. It's amusing and endearing, drawing a rare smile from me. Her eyes are wide and innocent, her blush deepening, and it makes me want her even more.

I take over from her, sliding the material down to my knees as I lower her gently onto her back. I slide her suit the rest of the way down her legs and off as I pull my shorts completely off as well.

There I am, fully exposed to her curious gaze. The way she bites her lower lip. The way her eyes dart to my throbbing length then back to my face. Damn, it's the sexiest thing I've ever seen.

I drag my fingers slowly up her stomach and back to her breasts. Leaning down, I take a nipple in my mouth, circling my tongue around the nipple until it's hard. I take it gently between my teeth as I twist the other nipple with my fingers.

I feel her gasp as the sensation floods her body and I know she's mine. I continue sucking on her breast as my right hand slides down her side to the crease of her leg. Then with the lightest of touch I drag my fingers over to her center and down into the fold of her pussy.

I feel her wetness as I moan in delight. Then I gently push my fingers inside her. The feeling of her surrounding my fingers is like finding the Holy Grail. She's tight and warm, gripping me in a way that's all consuming. Hell, I'm drowning and there's no way I'd want to be saved.

As I slide in deeper, she clenches around me. It's like she's pulling me in deeper, a silent plea for more. It's a battle cry I answer with enthusiasm. "You're so tight, Vi," I can't help but growl. "So wet... and all for me."

I thrust my fingers harder, faster. My inner hand brushes against her sweet spot, earning a gasp and a louder moan. I can't hold back the cocky smile that stretches my lips. There's something inherently powerful about having her writhing beneath me. Surrendering to my touch.

I slide my fingers out gently, but the look on her face says she's ready to kill me for taking my fingers out. She's a wreck under me, her whole body shaking with need. I can't help but chuckle. Sorry, sweetheart, but this is my game and I make the rules.

I align myself at her entrance, pressing just the tip in. She shudders beneath me, her eyes begging for more. Seeing her squirm under me, so desperate, is an intoxicating drug.

I push just a bit more in and her name tumbles from my lips. She's a symphony of whimpers, her hips trying to pull me in deeper. God, the control she's giving me is maddening.

"Ryan, please..." Her voice is a plea, shaky and desperate. It's music to my ears and fuel for my desire.

"Please what?" I tease, a wolfish grin splitting my face. She wants it, I know it, but I want to hear her words.

"Please... come inside me, Ryan," she moans, her voice barely a whisper over the sound of the rain.

Good girl. With permission granted, I push in, all the way. Her head lolls back, lost in the pleasure, and that's all the reward I need.

The feel of her wrapped around me sends a shiver down my spine. I bury my face in her neck, taking in her scent as I thrust deeper into her. Her hips under my hands are warm, responsive.

She clings to me like a lifeline, her legs hooked around my waist. I can't stop the low growl that escapes me. She's moaning my name, over and over. It's the sweetest damn sound I've ever heard.

I can feel every bit of her pussy, so warm, so tight. She's a hot, wet dream come true. I'm all in, and she's taking me, every inch.

"You look so good when you're taking it," I can't help but rumble into her ear. "You're doing so good, Vi, you feel so good." Those words, they're not my usual chatter, but then again, this isn't my usual gig.

She tastes like saltwater and sunshine, just the way I imagined. I latch onto a nipple, swirling my tongue around it. Her body shudders, and damn if that doesn't spur me on.

I've got one hand still pressed against her clit, forming circles. That always does the trick. But I'm not one to leave things half-done, so I grab her other tit with my free hand. Yeah, I'm resourceful like that.

As my fingers knead and pinch, my mouth is busy on her other breast. I bite down softly, then soothe it with my tongue. She's whimpering beneath me, fueling my fire.

Heat coils in my gut, like a damn spring ready to burst. I'm teetering on the edge, and I can tell she's right there with me. My mind is screaming at me to pull out, but my body... my body has other plans.

Her legs are wrapped around me like a damn boa constrictor. Not helping, Vi. Not helping at all.

Then, she gasps out my name, saying she's close, and it's like a match to a powder keg. I'm exploding, grunting so loud I'm sure the seagulls outside can hear. And I'm pouring myself into her, all control lost.

And then, like a magnet to steel, my lips find hers. I'm still buried inside her. Damn, it's heaven and hell all at once. We're there, lip-locked and breathless, for what feels like forever.

Then it hits me. That dreaded post-nut clarity. The little voice in my head screaming, *What the actual fuck, Ryan?* But right now? I couldn't care less.

Until... voices drift over the roaring waves. Voices are calling our names.

"Oh, shit." That's all I manage to spit out. Timing, you cruel bastard.

"Vi, we gotta move," I mutter against her lips. "Get your clothes on!"

She's quick, fumbling into her swimsuit and my shorts. I wrestle my wet shirt back on, my shorts follow suit.

Shit, shit, shit.

"Who is it, Ryan?" she whispers, glancing around, her voice all jittery. She slips my jacket on and zips it.

"No idea," I huff, "but we're on the 'most wanted' list, apparently."

Now there's this awkward tension. The whole 'We shouldn't have, but we totally did' vibe. What a bloody mess.

"Is it... Alec?" She's peering out the window, biting her lip.

Ah, hell! Not Alec!

The one guy I'd have to explain to that I just shagged his sister. I'm sure he'll be real understanding when I say it was a slip-up.

What a colossal screw-up.

Then there's a knock on the door. Yeah, shit just got real.

"Ryan? Vi? You guys in there?" Alec's voice echoes outside the shack.

Deep breath. Open the door. There stands Alec, drenched and panting.

"Are you guys okay?! I couldn't reach either of you for hours!"

My face is all kinds of red, I sputter, "Uh yeah, signals suck here, Alec."

He wrinkles his nose, "Smells kinda weird in here."

I scratch my head, "Uh yeah, must be the... seaweed." Smooth, Ryan. Real smooth.

Alec's eyes narrow slightly. He glances between Vi and me. Suspicion stirs.

"I see," he says, but it's clear he doesn't. Not yet. But something is off, and he knows it.

Damn it. I can already feel the awkward conversation that's coming.

16

THE LONG ROAD

VIOLET

The three of us squish into Alec's ridiculously flashy silver sports car. The tension is thick enough to cut with a butter knife. I'm sandwiched in the back, desperately trying to avoid making eye contact with anyone. Ryan's riding shotgun, his body rigid as a mannequin.

Alec breaks the silence, his eyes never leaving the road. "So, where'd you park your truck, Ryan?"

Ryan rubs his nape. "Ah, we had lunch at Cena Morada and decided to walk it off... you know, food coma. Our boards are still back at the lifeguard tower. Just drop me off and I'll go back for them."

Alec hums, a sound so flat it could serve as a pancake. "Thought you knew about the storm warnings."

Quick, Violet. Think. "Yeah, we did," I say. "But the waves, Alec, the waves were just too tempting. Ryan said it would be good for me to experience rough surf. But there was a downpour, very sudden, before we even got in the water."

Alec's eyes meet mine in the rear-view mirror. If looks could kill, I'd be six feet under. *Chill, brother bear.*

Sure, Alec is many things, but dumb isn't one of them. Our story, well, it's as shaky as a house of cards in a windstorm. The undeniable aroma of 'us' lingering in the lifeguard shack didn't do us any favors either.

My mind races, tripping over itself. What the hell happened? Ryan and I were just friends, right? Can we put this sex genie back in the bottle? The thought of it makes me tingle -- am I blushing?

Just focus, Violet. Not on Ryan's eyes, that's a danger zone. And for heaven's sake, avoid Alec's mirror stare too. Because right now, I'm caught between a rock and a hard, sexy place.

I can't let Alec find out. This... this whatever-it-was, must stay under wraps. Just when I start mentally crafting an escape plan, I catch Ryan's eyes flicking back to me.

Seriously? Look at the road, not at me. I swear I'm turning the exact shade of my red hair now.

You've got to love Alec, always throwing fuel on an already raging fire. He looks back in the rearview mirror and smirks. "Guess you two found your own way to ride out the storm, huh?"

Ryan, bless him, tries to play it cool. "Yeah, you know, nothing like an afternoon sitting in a cold, damp, musty old guard tower." But his poker face is worse than a dog playing fetch, and he's not fooling anyone.

In the backseat, I'm about two seconds from a full-blown panic attack. My heart is pounding against my rib cage like a desperate prisoner trying to break free.

"Surfing, huh?" Alec's tone is sharper than a butcher's knife. "You expect me to believe that?" He slams the gas pedal, and we jerk forward.

Ryan squares his shoulders. "Why the hell not, Alec? Last time I checked, you're not my babysitter."

Alec's lips tighten. "Maybe not, but you're hanging out with my sister, Ryan. That changes things."

"Oh, come off it, Alec!" Ryan's voice booms in the close space. "I was just trying to help her get better before the surf competition!"

"And the shack?" Alec's voice is harsh, low. "Smelled a little funky for a swim, don't you think?"

My heart stutters. Ryan, the idiot, starts sputtering. The car's speed matches my racing pulse. I feel like I might hurl at any moment.

"And you?" Alec turns his glare to me. My stomach clenches. "My own sister. You think I don't know when you're lying?"

Ryan's got nothing. His mouth moves, but no words come out. Just empty, useless air. And Alec's foot presses down harder on the gas. The engine roars as we speed down the empty highway, the streetlights blur in my vision.

"Enough!" I finally find my voice. It's shrill, panicked. Both men snap their jaws shut, surprised.

"Just cut it out, both of you!" My voice is a whip, snapping in the cramped car. My stomach churns with each vicious accusation they throw at each other.

"I don't know what you two are thinking," I hiss, "but whatever you imagine happened, it's not like that."

Alec's jaw clenches. He grips the steering wheel so hard his knuckles turn white. The car surges forward, faster, faster.

"I know my sister and my best friend well enough to see when they're lying," Alec grits out, each word like a shard of glass.

"Really, Alec?" My laugh is bitter, hollow. "You've got us all figured out, huh?"

Alec's silence is like a punch in the gut. He doesn't say a word, just keeps his eyes on the road, but I can see his jaw working.

"I'm not blind!" Alec's voice fills the car. The tension is too much, everything is too much. The seascape outside blurs with our speed.

"I'm an adult, Alec," I spit out, each word sharp, "I can make decisions for myself."

"But it's Ryan, Vi!" Alec barks, "My best friend, for Christ's sake!"

"And that makes me what?" Ryan's voice, at last, breaks through. It's raw, rough with hurt. "Just some wolf circling the flock?"

"You've always been a wolf, Ry," Alec retorts, venom coating his words. The car is a beast, rumbling, racing. "Always waiting for the right moment."

"And you?" Ryan's eyes are icy, locked onto Alec. "You've always been the overprotective big brother, haven't you? Controlling everyone else's life because you can't manage your own."

Alec's hands tighten around the steering wheel. The speedometer creeps higher. My heart feels like it's lodged in my throat, thudding wildly. They're too busy tearing each other apart to notice.

"Stop the car, Alec," I say, my voice trembling.

He doesn't. The speedometer climbs higher.

"Stop the damn car!" I scream, louder this time.

He finally does, the car screeching to a halt. As if on cue, I unfasten the seatbelt and tell Ryan to let me out. He complies and I bolt out into the cold rainy night.

Alec and Ryan are quick on my heels. "Vi, where are you going in this weather?!" Alec yells.

"I'm not dying in a car crash!" I yell back, making my way through the storm.

I keep marching on, but Alec's not having any of it. "Vi, just wait!"

Turning around, my eyes full of fire, I face him. "I'm not a kid, Alec!" I shout, "You don't get to play the big brother card anymore!"

"But you're my little sister," he starts, but I'm quick to cut him off.

"And you're my big, annoying brother who needs to mind his own fucking business!"

That shuts him up for a second. Ryan snaps his head toward me. Then back to Alec. But Alec doesn't stay quiet for long.

"I wonder what mom and dad will think about all this," he sneers. That's a low blow, even for him.

"You're kidding, Alec? Really?" Ryan's voice cuts through the tension like a hot knife. The storm rages on around us, mirroring our own storm of words.

Alec turns to him, smug as a cat with a mouse. "Our parents picked out the perfect match for our Vi. Rich, charming, prestigious. The whole package."

I snort. "We aren't in medieval times, Alec! I'm not marrying some guy just because our folks think it's a good idea."

"They've already chosen, Violet. You've got no choice." Alec's voice is cold, sharper than the winter air.

"No choice?" My laugh is hollow. "Oh, you've got it so wrong."

"Tell him, Vi. Tell him who they've chosen for you." The grin on Alec's face is downright malicious.

"Cole," I spit out the name like it is poison. "They want me to marry Cole."

I can see the shock on Ryan's face, clear as day, even in the storm. His lips part in surprise. "Cole? Seriously?"

"Oh, I'm deadly serious, dear Ryan." Alec's tone is gleeful. "Welcome to our family drama."

"Back in the car. Now!" Alec's yell cuts through the storm. Maybe he's raising his voice because of the weather. Or maybe he just wants to yell.

Fuming, I stomp back into the car. Same spot as before. My clothes, still soaked, stick to the seat. I'm freezing. I'm angry. I'm... I'm going to be sick tomorrow. Ugh.

Once we're all settled in, Alec glances at me in the rearview mirror. "Whatever happened between you two," he begins, his voice dangerously low, "never happened. Got it? Because she has a date tomorrow night."

"A date?" The question slips out of me before I can stop it.

I catch Ryan's eye in the dim light of the car. He looks as stunned as I feel.

Alec doesn't even glance our way. "You know we're in debt. If you don't want to lose everything our parents have built, you have to marry Cole. That's the agreement."

Ryan whips his head towards Alec. "What agreement?"

The question hangs in the air, unanswered, as Alec turns his attention back to the road.

"You can't do that to her, Alec!" Ryan's voice is a storm itself, thundering over the howl of the wind outside. "She's your sister! How can you be okay with something like this?"

Alec doesn't react for a moment. Then, slowly, he turns his head towards Ryan. There's a hard edge to his voice when he finally replies. "Okay with something like what? You're lucky you're my best friend. If you were just some random guy…"

He lets his voice trail off, leaving the rest to our imagination. Ryan raises an eyebrow. "What then, huh?"

I've had enough. "Just shut up, both of you!" My shout drowns out both of their voices.

"Now that we've gone down Pacific Coast Highway 20 miles in the wrong direction… Turn this car around and take Ryan back to his truck! NOW DAMMIT!"

It's like dropping a pebble in a pond - suddenly, all the noise stops. The car falls silent, except for the sound of the rain hitting the roof.

I sink back into my seat, crossing my arms over my chest. They both shut up, their eyes back on the road. Alec turns the car around, but the tension doesn't disappear.

I sigh and glance out the window, watching the drops of rain race each other down the glass.

This is going to be a long road back. And a long night.

17

THE PUPPET

VIOLET

Oh my God, he didn't. He really didn't. But there he is, Ryan, outside my window at two in the morning, throwing rocks like he's auditioning for a rom-com role. I rush to the window, peeking through the curtains.

"Ryan! What are you doing here?"

"We need to talk," he whispers back, his eyes gleaming in the moonlight. Typical Ryan. Always dramatic.

"I can't let you in," I say, trying to sound firm. But let's face it, my knees are wobbling like jelly, and not just because he's out there looking up in my window.

"Who said anything about letting me in? I'll just climb," he says, a cheeky grin on his face. And then he starts climbing. Like Spider-Man, but hotter.

"Are you insane?" I gasp, my eyes wide as saucers. But I can't help but watch him, mesmerized by the grace and strength of his movements. Who knew a man climbing up the side of a house could be so sexy?

"I've been called worse."

I open the window wider, and he climbs in. There's something in his gaze, something urgent, something desperate.

Something that tells me this is more than just a late-night booty call.

"What's going on?" I ask, my voice trembling.

"We need to talk about us," he says, his voice serious, his eyes intense. "About what happened today."

I swallow hard, my mind racing. What does he want? What does he expect?

"You, me, Alec," he continues, his voice low and urgent. "We need to figure this out. We need to be honest with each other."

Alright, this boy needs to cool his jets, but of course, I'm the one who needs a bath. Ryan's watching me, those intense eyes burning a hole through me, and all I can think about is tomorrow night. Cole. Ugh.

"I-uh, I need to sleep. To take a bath,"

"To meet Cole tomorrow?" he asks, his voice dripping with disdain. It's funny, really, how his name sounds like an insult when Ryan says it.

I nod, feeling guilty and trapped. "I mean... it's not like I have a choice. Can we talk after that?"

Ryan just nods, his jaw clenched, his eyes dark. "Alright."

I turn on the water, glancing back at Ryan. He's still watching me, a little too intently for comfort. Oh, this boy needs boundaries.

"Turn around, perv!"

He chuckles, this deep, rich sound that makes my stomach do flips, and he turns around obediently. The bathtub fills with water and bubbles, luxurious and warm.

I get undressed and slip into the bath, the water enveloping me. I can hear Ryan talking, but his words are lost in the distance.

"I mean, are you actually going--" he starts, but I can't make out the rest. He's too far away, and he's whispering, probably worried about my folks hearing us. As if we haven't already crossed a thousand lines.

"Can't hear you!" I call out, pretending to cup my ear.

Ryan turns around, his eyes widening as he realizes I'm in the bath. He hesitates for just a second before he moves closer, leaning against the door frame. I can see the muscles in his arms, his strong shoulders, and I remind myself to breathe.

"What?" he asks, his voice a little louder now. He's still being cautious, but at least I can hear him.

I pretend to think about it, tapping my finger against my chin. "What was that you were saying about Cole?"

Ryan's face darkens, and he steps closer still. "I was asking if you were really going to follow through with that weasel. And this bizarre plan?"

I shrug, playing with the bubbles, avoiding his eyes. "Like Alec said, it's not like I have a choice."

Ryan stays silent for a moment, and I can feel his eyes on me, heavy and intense. I look up, meeting his gaze, and something in his eyes makes my heart race.

"Violet," he says, his voice soft and serious. "You always have a choice."

And then he's moving closer, his hands on the edge of the tub, his eyes locked on mine. I can feel the heat of him, the pull of him, and I know I'm lost.

Ryan's grin should be illegal. "Can I join you?" he asks, like it's the most normal thing in the world to climb into a bubble bath with a girl you're not supposed to be with.

"Are you insane, Ryan?"

"I need to have a bath as well," he says, feigning innocence. Oh please, like anyone's buying that act.

I can't help but laugh. "Well, I guess my bathtub is big enough. But no funny business," I warn, trying to sound stern. Yeah, right. Who am I kidding? I think I gave the same warning in the guard tower to no avail.

His eyes are on me, sharp and intense, as he unbuttons his shirt. I watch, transfixed, as he works the buttons and material free. My heart's racing, beating so quickly I'm sure it's about to escape my chest.

This is crazy. This is insane. This is... exactly what I want.

He's down to his pants now, and I'm trying not to stare, but it's impossible. He's beautiful, and I can't look away.

"You sure about this?"

Am I sure? No, not really. But do I want it? More than anything.

I nod, biting my lip, a thrill of anticipation running through me.

He smiles, and it's like the sun coming out. "Okay then," he says, and he steps out of his pants, moving towards the tub.

I watch, mesmerized, as he slips into the water. His body moves gracefully, the muscles in his back and arms flexing. He settles in across from me, his eyes on mine, a smile playing on his lips.

I smile back, a little giddy, a little nervous, a lot excited.

The bubble bath takes on a playful life of its own as Ryan and I start splashing water at each other. Laughter fills the room as water and bubbles fly. It's silly, it's fun, and it's the most alive I've felt in a long time.

"Hey, watch it!" I squeal, as Ryan sends a particularly large wave of bubbly water in my direction.

"Make me,"

Oh, it's on now.

I send a wave back at him, and he laughs, trying to dodge it. We're acting like kids, and I love it. The bubbles are our cover, hiding our naked bodies. Allowing us to be free and playful without worrying about anything else.

But as the water settles and our laughter fades, the mood shifts.

Ryan's looking at me, his eyes dark and serious, his wet hair slicked back. I can feel the heat in his gaze.

"Don't look!" I tease, splashing water toward Ryan's face. I conveniently forget the fact that we've already seen everything there is to see. He retaliates, sending a cascade of bubbly water my way.

"You're going to let the water spill over," I laugh as I pull back. I watch as the water teeters dangerously close to the edge of the tub.

"I've got it all under control."

I know he's up to something. He reaches for the washcloth, soap in hand. "Let me wash you," he says, his voice low.

Oh, he's good.

I pretend to consider it, tilting my head, feigning reluctance. "Well, if you insist."

18

SPLISH SPLASH

VIOLET

I move so now I'm sitting on his lap, my back against his chest. He starts to wash my body, his hands moving slowly, massaging every inch of me. The sensation is so exquisite I can't help but let out a contented sigh.

"God, that's nice," I practically moan, feeling his fingers brushing over my hard nipples.

He just smiles, continuing his work. I turn around so that he can massage my legs and feet, sinking into the pleasure of his touch.

"How's that?"

"Heavenly," I reply, sinking lower into the water. I'm completely lost in the sensation as I lean my head back against his chest.

He smiles wide, satisfaction in his eyes. "Good."

I bite down on my lip, though Ryan can't see, and gently roll my hips backward. He groans when I brush against him.

"What are you doing?" he asks.

"Me? Nothing," I say innocently.

I rub my ass against his cock causing him to moan again.

"Tease," he mumbles.

"Am not."

It doesn't take much more of that for Ryan to become fully erect again.

And I don't stop. I move so that his cock slips gently between my cheeks.

"Oh god, Violet,"

Ryan sucks his breath in sharply. At the sound, I turn my head to see his longing look, flushed to his ears. I want it as much as he does, yet I am too embarrassed to outright admit it.

So I say nothing and twist around to look up at him, chewing my bottom lip. Ryan's eyes trail down to my lips, and he leans closer. I tilt my head back and close my eyes.

I don't even need to tell him to kiss me because his lips are latching onto mine. Ryan grumbles a deep moan into my mouth and bucks his hips. My attention is drawn to his proudly standing cock that points directly at me. I moan back into his mouth even louder, and Ryan rubs his cock against my clit.

I wrap my arms over his shoulders and face him on my knees. His lips find mine once again, and water moves around us. His cock is sliding up and down around my midsection as I grind.

He opens his mouth, inviting me in, and I slide my tongue in. Our tongues swirl around as he grunts in my mouth, and my breasts press against him.

I rub Ryan's cock between my thighs, gliding my soaked pussy up and down on it. The sight of Ryan's large, throbbing cock between my legs finally drives me past my breaking point. I can't stop imagining it inside of me.

"Ryan, please fuck me..." I throatily whisper, wrapping my hands around his neck.

Ryan lets out another low chuckle, his laughter rumbles right against my breasts. I squeak when I feel his cock twitch in response to my excitement. I squeak again when Ryan begins peppering my throat with countless bites and kisses.

"Well," Ryan whispers against my lips, smiling, "Your wish is my command, princess." And with that, Ryan buries his head into my shoulder. Lightly biting to muffle his throaty groan, he pushes his cock all the way inside me.

My thighs quiver, and I let out a tiny groan. Every nerve in my body is being burned by the sweetest, most electrifying fire I have ever felt. I wrap my legs around the small of Ryan's back and gyrate my hips against him. I want him to fill me with his magic wand again.

"Oh...Ryan..." I moan. Ryan thrusts into me sharply once before returning to his regular tempo. Even while we're fucking, Ryan still loves messing around with me. "You're so annoying ..." I whine, wanting him to go harder again.

"Really?" Ryan whispers, throwing me another innocent smile as if he isn't balls-deep inside me right now. He latches his mouth onto my nipple and suddenly holds me tight against him, thrusting hard into me again.

I throw my neck back and yell my whispered whines to the air. I curse myself for talking smack to Ryan. Even while he's making a *smack smack smack* sound out of our entangled bodies in the bathtub.

My pale hands are digging into the taut muscles of Ryan's bronze back. Ryan's dark hands dig into my fair-skinned waist like it's fresh fruit after a long famine. Ryan's thrusts grow sloppier, and my bounces grow wilder.

The bathwater ricochets around us. We only hold onto each other harder, slippery from the water. Desperately not wanting the other to slip out of our grip.

Ryan holds me tight against him. I loop my legs around Ryan's legs so hard I'm starting to feel my circulation cut off.

"Fuck...Violet..."

Ryan spews out against my shoulder. Smack smack smack. "Fuck...tell me you're mine..." He begs in a throaty rasp. One of his hands finds its way to my ass and squeezes it for all it's worth. "Ah!" I shriek.

His voice fills my mind with imagery of Ryan pumping every last drop of his spunk into me. "Yes!" I concede. "Yes!" I pant as Ryan fucks my brains out.

I grip the edges of the tub. Ryan locks one arm around my waist and holds tightly. I begin to move, rolling my hips smoothly over his lap and letting his thick length pump in and out of me.

Neither of us is going to last long, but it's probably for the best. I've barely started to move, and already the water is beginning to slop and slosh over the side of the tub. I don't hold back, starting to bounce with the current of the water and ride him in earnest.

Beneath me, his body spasms.

"God," he gasps. "Vi, I-I'm gonna... shit, you gotta..."

His hand scrambles over my thigh, finding its apex and searching for my clit. He finds it and circles it deftly. He jerks his hips against my downward thrusts, forcing me furiously toward my climax.

It spirals spectacularly out of me as I cry sharply into the humidity of the bathroom. My fingers tighten hard against the edges of the tub. I slam my hips down hard, holding them there while my pussy clenches around him.

He follows closely behind me, emptying his balls into my belly and letting me milk him dry.

When it's over for both of us, we sit for a moment, basking in the heady glow of our pleasure and catching our breath. His chest is damp but solid and broad, and he traces his fingers idly over my side as he goes soft inside me.

"You okay?" he finally asks, his voice soft and full of genuine concern.

"More than okay," I chuckle, leaning back against him. "You?"

"Perfect," he whispers, planting a gentle kiss on my shoulder. "But we probably need to get out before we become human prunes."

With a shared laugh, we reluctantly climb out of the tub, our legs a bit wobbly and our bodies still tingling. Ryan grabs towels, and we take turns drying each other off, the intimacy of the moment far from lost.

After we're dressed, Ryan looks at me with a soft expression. His eyes are filled with something tender and real. "I should get going," he says, but there's hesitation in his voice, as if he's reluctant to leave.

I nod, understanding but feeling a pang of sadness. "Yeah, I guess you should."

We share one more lingering kiss at the window. Then he's gone, leaving me with a warm glow in my chest and a smile that won't quite leave my face.

19

THE MORNING AFTER

VIOLET

Morning comes quicker than I'd like, the stubborn sun peeking through the crack in my curtains. My body feels heavy with exhaustion, each muscle crying out for just five more minutes of sleep. I manage to heave myself out of bed, every movement a challenge.

I reach for my phone, desperate to tell Alissa about yesterday's excitement. The half of a surfing lesson, the El Manada gang, the Cena Morada. And can't forget Hurricane Gemma storming the diner.

The walk back to the beach, the storm moving in, the love in the tower, then the fallout with Alec. Later the love in the tub.

It's hard to believe all of that happened in one day. No wonder my body aches all over. And now tonight, I go out with Cole. Yuck! Fuck Yuck!

I can't type all the details in a text. I need to tell her in person.

> *Alissa, what are you doing?*
> *You have to come over quick.*
> *I have so much to tell you.*

What is it?
Did something happen?
Are you alright?

I wish she'd just say yes.

Too much to text.
You have to come over.
Just come up to my room
when you get here. And hurry!

So I wait, going over all the details in my mind. I can't leave out one detail.

The doorbell rings and Mom lets her in. I hear Alissa running up the steps, her long legs taking two steps at a time. I open the bedroom door just as she's about to knock.

"Get in here. You are not going to believe what I am about to tell you!"

20

THE DATE

VIOLET

There's a knock at the door, so polite it makes me want to throw a book at it. But I put on my best fake smile instead and open it. There stands Cole. Slicked back hair, a fancy suit, and a smile so shiny it could blind you. He looks like he just stepped out of a cologne ad.

"You ready, Violet?" His voice is smooth as honey, his eyes sparkling with enthusiasm. I roll my eyes, something Alec might do. I wonder if that was a subconscious decision. I've no desire to let Cole think he's got this in the bag.

"Sure, let's get this over with." I slam the door behind me, leaving no room for response.

In the car, he's all charm and compliments, like he's reading from a handbook titled 'How to Woo a Woman in Ten Easy Steps'. It's irritatingly amusing. I play along, batting my eyelashes and giving non-committal answers.

The drive to the restaurant is short, but not short enough. The restaurant he chooses is all white tablecloths and crystal glasses. I sit opposite him, feeling out of place.

He smiles across the table, ready to dive into small talk. I let him ramble, the sound of his voice a monotonous drone in the background. I poke at my food, ignoring his attempts at engaging me.

The food is great, but my appetite has abandoned me. I nod in all the right places, giving him the illusion of a pleasant conversation. The whole scene is as fake as a three-dollar bill. It's hard to swallow, just like the overpriced lobster on my plate.

The date drags on, each minute crawling slower than the last. His stories become more grandiose, his laugh louder. He doesn't notice my lack of interest, or if he does, he doesn't care. I guess that's how it goes when you're an obscenely rich heir who's used to getting what he wants.

Finally, the check arrives and it's time to leave. He insists on paying, playing the part of the perfect gentleman to the bitter end. We step back into the cold night, the silence in the car hanging heavy between us. My monstrous house looms in the distance, the end of this torturous evening in sight.

The moment the car stops, I'm out of it and heading towards the house. No goodbye, no thank you. Just the slamming of the car door echoing behind me. It's a perfect end to a perfectly horrible date. The grand reveal of my future. The loveless existence that awaits me. Oh, joy.

The house is all abuzz when I step through the front door. I can hear the voices before I even take off my jacket. I rub my temples, preparing for the storm that's about to hit.

I round the corner to the living room and there they are, all smiles and joy. It's like a festive parade and I'm the reluctant guest of honor. My brother Alec is holding court, gleaming like a newly polished silver spoon. Beside him, my parents nod approvingly, their faces mirroring his satisfaction.

Mom looks up, her eyes bright. "Oh, there she is!" She stands up, all motherly pride and enthusiasm. The way she's looking at me, it's like I've just won a Nobel prize or something.

Dad grins, the corners of his eyes crinkling. "How was it, Violet?" he asks, like he's enquiring about a field trip. His question was demanding a response for sure.

I shrug, trying to play it cool. But my voice is flat when I answer, "It was okay." What else am I supposed to say?

My parents exchange a glance, their eyebrows furrowing in unison. Alec clears his throat, obviously playing big brother slash peacekeeper slash marriage broker. "Cole is a good man, Vi," he insists, his voice sincere. It's like he genuinely believes what he's saying. He doesn't know, doesn't understand.

Suddenly, I see him everywhere. Ryan. His smile, his laughter, the way his eyes crinkle when he's genuinely happy. He's a constant presence in my mind, a phantom haunting me. A stark contrast to the hollow pageant happening in the room.

I plaster a smile on my face, nodding along like a bobblehead doll. Mom gushes about color schemes and flower arrangements. "I love lilacs," she says. "You should have lilacs." Of course, her lilacs, her wedding, her dream.

"Vi," Dad calls me back from my thoughts, waving his hands for emphasis. "You and Cole, at a beach for your honeymoon. Imagine!" He sighs like he's picturing it himself. My stomach churns.

"And children," my mother chimes in. She clasps her hands together like she's already knitting baby booties. "Beautiful little ones running around." I take a discreet deep breath, pretending to share in her excitement. Inside, though, it feels like I'm choking on sandpaper.

I raise an eyebrow, as a daring thought crosses my mind. I lean forward, resting my chin on my hand. "And what if I don't want kids, Mom?" I ask, my voice oozing innocence. The room goes quiet. The only sound is the clock ticking, its every tick screaming 'traitor'.

Mum blinks at me, completely thrown off. Dad drops his hands, mouth opening and closing like a goldfish out of water. And Alec, bless him, looks like he's just been slapped with a wet fish.

"You don't mean that," Alec finally blurts out, attempting to laugh it off. I look at him, head tilted to one side. Do I not?

Before I can add more fuel to the fire, Mum jumps in. "Oh, she's just joking,"

They're envisioning a power couple, the golden duo. Cole and Violet, saving the family's reputation and fortune.

"You and Cole will be invincible," Alec says, trying to rally the mood. "He's a business tycoon. You're smart. It's a match made in heaven."

Oh, I just can't resist this one. I let out a dramatic sigh, fanning myself with my hand. "Oh, Alec," I murmur, batting my eyelashes at him. "I didn't know you had such romantic notions. You really think business contracts are what love stories are made of?"

Alec's face flushes red, caught between embarrassment and frustration. Mom and Dad exchange another one of their glances. And me? I'm just enjoying the show.

My laugh is raw and bitter. "You guys are bonkers if you think I'm playing along in this absurd soap opera." My voice drips with disbelief, while Dad's face hardens like I've declared war. Well, maybe I have.

His hand slams on the table, rattling the china. "You WILL fall in line, Violet!" His voice booms, making the chandelier quiver. But me? I don't flinch.

I lean against the table and cross my arms over my chest. "Maybe you should have thought about that before losing all of our money to gambling!"

Just as the atmosphere grows tenser, Mom acts as the pacifier, the water to Dad's fire. She places a hand on his chest, an unspoken signal to cool it. She then turns to me, her voice soft but steady.

"Vi, you're just scared, dear," she coos, like I'm some child lost in a crowd. "Cole is affluent, comes from a high-status family. It's a golden opportunity."

And there it is. The money and the status. So, I lay it out, blunt as a baseball bat. "So, it all boils down to cash and reputation, huh?"

My accusation hangs heavy in the air. Dad's eyes flash but Mom doesn't back down. She meets my gaze, holding it firmly. "Yes. Yes, it does. His family's financial support is vital for us. And Cole, he adores you. He's willing to settle our debts forever."

I feel the bile rise in my throat, a bitter taste of truth. Money, power, prestige. It's a game, and I am just another pawn. I'm supposed to thank them, maybe even curtsy to Cole for his grand benevolence.

Well, not today. Not ever.

I don't say a word. What's the point? The script is set. But they forget one thing - I'm not their puppet.

Stifling a sigh, Dad rubs his temples as if warding off a migraine. "Violet, listen," he begins, tone softer now, maybe understanding the storm within me. His eyes hold a plea, an unspoken regret. He's never been good with words.

"I've failed as a father, haven't I?" He doesn't wait for my response. "We've had our share of good days, but recently... it's just been hard times." It's the first time he's admitted it. Our family ship isn't sailing, it's sinking.

He takes a deep breath, a silent prayer perhaps before he drops the truth bomb. "The company... it's in shambles. We're drowning in debt, and the sharks are circling."

He lets the revelation sink in, the magnitude of their desperation laid bare. And for a moment, we all sit in silence. The ticking of the grandfather clock is a mocking reminder of time slipping away.

Mom's hand finds mine across the table, her grip tight. "Cole's family is our lifeline, Vi," she whispers, her voice almost cracking. "And Cole... he genuinely cares for you. This isn't just a business transaction for him."

Alec, who's been quieter than a church mouse, finally pipes up. "Vi, it sucks. But it's our only shot."

With a heavy sigh, I rake my fingers through my hair. My family, the people I'd fight for, are asking me to surrender. To a fate penned by others. To a life I don't want.

I take a moment to look at them. At Dad, the stoic figurehead, now vulnerable. At Mom, always the peacekeeper, holding back tears. And at Alec, the golden boy, caught in a situation he didn't ask for.

I breathe and inhale the weight of their hopes. Then exhale the cloud of my defiance. One look at their faces, and I know, this isn't a demand. It's a desperate plea.

I don't say anything. Not yet. But I take another breath, acknowledging the crossroads I'm at. One path leads to Cole, the golden cage. The other, a storm with no assurance of survival.

I guess it's time to see what kind of diamond this pressure is going to create.

"And um... He is waiting for you in the garden, Vi." Alec mumbles with his arms crossed.

What?!

21

THE GARDEN

VIOLET

I move past my brother toward the garden. I am aware that my arms and legs are stiff, not moving together but jerking along. *I really am a puppet on a string.*

As my eyes adjust to the outdoor lighting, I see Cole seated at the long marble table, his back to me. I scoff at this view of his creepy hair and the back of his neck. *Ryan's strong, bare shoulders flash into my mind, and I blink away the image.*

"So, you have something more to discuss?" I say bitterly as I approach him.

"Violet, I assume your parents have explained the situation to you. You know that I have always admired you, loved you from a distance. I am prepared to do everything in my power to make you the happiest woman in the world," Cole sputters. He rises to face me.

"And how do you propose to do that Cole?" I shoot back in response.

Cole ignores me and my remark and presses on as if reading from a script. "As you know, my investments in recent years have been prosperous. I have the means to keep you and your family safe and secure in your stature and position permanently.

"The Bailey name will continue without tarnish or scandal. You will have the prestige of my position, with every comfort available to you. Anything you desire will be within your grasp," he offers.

Cole steps forward and extends a Tiffany blue box tied with a gold cord. "I chose this for you, but please know that any ring in the world can be yours if you accept this proposal."

"Proposal? Don't you mean contract?" I spit, reaching for the box which I do not open.

"So that's it? No paper to sign, no list of demands, no pledge to make? What do you expect me to say, Cole? This all seems to have been arranged around me without my knowledge."

And then he moves in close, his face inches from mine, the scent of his cologne fresh and stinging to my senses. I lower my eyes to avoid looking directly at him.

"I expect you to do the right thing for everyone, as you have always done. I understand you may need some time to adjust to the idea, but I'm sure you realize what is at stake here. Not just for you and me, but for your family, Violet. Family is everything."

Cole puts his hand on my shoulder, and I involuntarily shrug and shudder at his touch.

"I have some business on the east coast. I leave tomorrow for a few weeks. I'm sure Mrs. Bailey will be eager to assist you with wedding arrangements and you can fill me in when I return.

"Give my regards to Alec and your parents. I need to prepare for my early flight," Cole squeezes my shoulder before he retreats through the side gate. The only thing missing from his medieval performance is a suit of armor.

I stare at the box and let out my breath with a sound I can't identify as a laugh or a sob.

RYAN

Ah, the joys of being left unread. I have texted Vi countless times today, but radio silence. Maybe they've snatched her phone away, a new-age grounded punishment.

Even Alec hasn't replied. My best friends, ladies and gentlemen, champions of communication.

I have no choice now, do I? Time for a good old visit. Might as well walk into the lion's den and face whatever roar they can muster.

I don't drive up to their fancy mansion. Instead, I park my car blocks away. Stealth mode activated, a regular ninja.

Strolling towards their fortress, hands buried in my pockets, I shiver. Yeah, it's freezing, and yeah, I should've worn a jacket. But hey, sacrifices must be made for the art of espionage, right?

They're my friends, after all. No amount of yelling or secret arrangements can change that. Plus, a little drama never hurt anyone. Well, except for my sanity, maybe.

As I reach their house, all the exterior lights are ablaze creating a larger than usual circle of light to avoid. A deceptive little glow, isn't it? Cover the mess inside with a warm façade. My lips twitch into a smirk as I slip into the side shadows to approach the house from the rear.

A look at their house, and my head's a rollercoaster of last night's memories. Those breathless whispers. Damn, the girl knows how to make a guy lose his mind.

The thought of Violet surrendering to marry him, Mr. Big Bucks. With his polished shoes and pristine suits. What does he have that I don't? Except slicked back ugly hair. Ugh, the guy gives me the icks.

But this is Violet we're talking about. The girl I've watched face the world with a sassy smile and a pocket full of comebacks. And the look in her eyes, the fire that refuses to die, no way will she bow down to some gold-plated marriage deal.

They've thrown a curveball at her, sure. But if there's one thing I know about Vi, she bats those away for breakfast. Yeah, she's one tough cookie. And I'm standing here in the cool of night, hoping she won't crumble.

I stop short in the shadows of the garden, taking in a sight to sour my mood. Vi is standing in the garden. And there's Mr. Slick-back-hair himself, Cole, all too close to her.

My fists clench on instinct, the urge to deck him right in his perfectly chiseled jaw. Or better, a swift kick to the balls, for good measure.

I see him lean in closer, and that's when my blood really starts to boil. It's like watching a nature show where the predator zeroes in on the prey. Back off, pretty boy. She's not your damn dinner.

I watch and wait for Vi to brush him away, but she doesn't. And then I see the box, the offering, the lure, and my heart beats louder in my chest. *This can't be real.*

Why the hell should this even bother me, right? It's not like there's some undying love between Vi and me. Our times together were just... tension, fun, temptation. Nothing at all to do with feelings.

But damn it, how could she do this? She was just venting about how much she despised the guy. She claimed she'd never marry him. And then she just... changes her mind?

What's this about an agreement anyway? Does she really love him? I swear, I'm about two seconds from rearranging slick-back's perfect smile.

So, that's why she wasn't answering my texts. I was nothing more than a distraction for her. Nice one, Vi. Alec's little innocent sister is just another vixen after all.

Maybe it's best if I keep my distance. Her family isn't exactly handing out invites for Sunday brunch.

My hands are shaking like I'm on a caffeine overload. I curl them into fists. Why can't I just get it into my skull - she's not mine. I have no claim on her. She is nothing to me.

She's said her piece, made her choice. Destined to be some rich dude's trophy wife.

Turning on my heel, I head back to my car.

22

SURFING COMING UP NEXT

RYAN

The rows of XX's on the calendar tell me the surfing competition is tomorrow. Sleep has been a no-show the past weeks, the jerk. I've gone cold turkey on seeing her. Or him. Alec has turned into a clingy ex-girlfriend, my phone buzzing like a mad bee. I toy with the block button.

I get it. Sleep is important, all for the sake of the big show tomorrow. But my groove has left the building Elvis style. Maybe my groove caught a flight with sleep. I can't focus, and I definitely can't shake off the persistent itch at the back of my mind.

Come on, Ryan. Focus. Get your surf together. Rules. The bane of my existence. Can't sleep, can't eat. And the worst one - can't call Vi. Gritting my teeth, I throw a punch at the air. Man, I need a distraction. But my stubborn brain only circles back to one thing: Violet.

Scoring. Judges don't just count how many waves surfers catch. They're looking at the best moves, the size of the wave and the style. Yeah, even in a wetsuit, style counts. And of course, making the best of the wave you catch.

Priority rules. It's like a wet version of king of the hill. When the match starts, everyone is equal. The one closest to the wave's peak gets the next ride. Catch a wave, and you move to the end of the line.

Interference is a no-go. Don't ride a wave in front of the surfer with priority. Or mess with his scoring run. You'll be assessed a penalty, which is usually one less wave score.

Safety is the big rule. It's mandatory to strap that leash on your ankle. No leash, no game. No one wants to be the dude whose board clocks someone in the head.

Pills. My mind snaps to Mom's sleeping aid, which I usually don't need, but tonight is a special case. I sneak them from her bathroom, two small white promises of rest.

I still can't sleep. I feel like a kid on Christmas Eve, only there will be no presents in the morning. Just waves and judges. Maybe it's anxiety. Nah, not me. But, well, maybe a little nerves. No big deal.

Swallow the pills, chase them with a swig of water. Here's to a good night's sleep. If the bloody things work, that is.

In the dim light of early dawn, I roll out of bed. The damn pills only bought me a few hours of rest. Time to prep, time to focus. I probably look like a raccoon got in a scrap with a grizzly. No time to verify, though.

Mirror's there, but who's got time for vanity? Not this guy. The bathroom light flickers on, and I catch sight of the shower. Steam and hot water, first things first. The tiles are cold against my feet, a sharp contrast to the scalding water I let fall over me.

Each drop is like a damn wake-up call, but it's necessary. The water cleanses the sleep, clears the mind. My fingers find the shampoo bottle, familiar and slick. Suds form, run down my body, and circle the drain. All part of the cycle.

Wrapped in a towel, still damp, I saunter to the kitchen. No fancy breakfast for me. A plain slice of toast, a smear of peanut butter. Energy, that's what it's about. I need fuel for the waves, for the performance. I chew mechanically, my mind elsewhere.

In the corner, the surfboard beckons. My old reliable, slick and waxed to perfection. My hands trace over it, checking for imperfections. But she's flawless, ready for the show. My fingers work deftly, securing the leash. Safety first, even when there's fun to be had.

I turn on my favorite playlist, some song about lost love. *Yeah, right.* I crank the volume up to let the beats fill the room. *I don't care. It's my heart on the line.*

Decked out in my wetsuit, I'm a vision of focus. Tight, neoprene second skin. It restricts, it protects. It's not about comfort, it's about function. Zipper goes up, with a satisfying sound, another task done.

Next, the wax. The sweet smell fills my nostrils. I rub it on the board to make sure it's ready to grip. No slips out there today in front of the crowd.

Bags packed, board under my arm, I head out the door. The sun is barely over the horizon. The early bird gets the worm, or in my case, the wave. It's all about timing, you know.

The keys jingle in my hand as I unlock my truck and stash the board in the back with care. It's like a part of me, after all. I can't be reckless with it. The engine roars to life, and I'm on my way.

Music blares through the speakers, a backdrop to my thoughts. I let it wash over me to drown out the noise in my head. I don't care, remember? Not my problem.

The drive is a blur, just like everything else. Before I know it, I'm there. The ocean calls my name. Time to put on a show, time to ride. All else, all worries, are left behind. After all, why would I care?

As I step onto the sand, the cool granules between my toes, I let that thought sink in. Today, it's about me. The waves. The thrill. The rest of it doesn't matter. Not today.

The sun is fully up now, bathing the beach in warm light. The day is going to be a scorcher. The perfect day for a surfing competition, if you ask me. But nobody did.

I glance at my watch. *7:45 AM. T-minus 15 minutes 'til showtime.* Surfers, fans, sponsors – they're all trickling in, waiting for the magic to begin. Me? I'm just leaning against my truck, taking in the scene.

A few friendly faces pop over to chit-chat. Nothing deep, just the usual pre-competition banter. Predictions, bravado, surf lingo. I contribute my share of nods and grunts. I don't want to come off as the rude one.

Dave, the event organizer, waddles up to me. This guy is as round as he is tall. He always has a smile on his face and a joke on his lips. Not the best ones, but who's judging?

"The swell is gonna be gnarly today, Ryan," he chirps. I flash him a thumbs-up, the universal sign for 'whatever you say, buddy'.

Then, there's Lisa, the surfer chick and part-time photographer. She keeps trying to get me to pose for her *Surfers of Southern California* calendar. Not my style, but she gives me a wave from across the crowd. I wave back of course. I'm all cordial here on the sand.

Kiddos are running around, their laughter blending with the waves. The sights and sounds remind me why I love the surf. The joy, the excitement is pure, innocent and infectious. The surf helps me forget all the bullshit life can pile on.

Suddenly, I spot her, without even realizing I was searching for her. Standing at the fringe of the crowd, her ginger hair flaming in the morning breeze. It's her, no mistake. She's here.

Ah, hell. I didn't think she'd show. I almost wish she hadn't. It's easier to pretend when she's out of sight. But she's here now. And me? I'm not ready for that kind of emotional tsunami. Not today.

She's wearing her black and green wetsuit. The shade of green matches her eyes which are scanning the crowd, seeking, searching. *Looking for me?* Maybe. I don't know.

Should I go over, say hello? Nah, too complicated. I lean harder against the truck and try to blend into the background. Good luck with that, Ryan, you're a 6'2" surfer at a surfing competition.

Instead, I let my gaze wander to the ocean. The waves are picking up. It's almost time.

My heart's pounding like a rabbit. Not nerves, no. It's her. *Damn her*.

But the waves are calling, and I can't ignore them. I hoist my board, run a hand through my hair. No matter what, I won't let her distract me.

I mean, why would I? It's not my loss, remember?

I head toward the water. But not before stealing one last glance her way. She hasn't seen me yet. Good.

It's time to surf, to ride the waves, to lose myself in the rhythm of the ocean, to do what I love, what I was born to do.

23

READY TO GO

VIOLET

Okay, here I am. Point Dume in Malibu. The sun is a bright ball of mischief, playing peekaboo with the Pacific. A glorious day, isn't it?

The surf competition's already bustling with life. A sea of heads is bobbing around, chattering, squealing, whatnot. Is it even 8:00 yet? God, these surf people wake up way too early.

Did I mention the smell? Sea salt and sunscreen, sure. But also, the faint tang of excitement and anticipation. Funny how those things have a smell. Or is that just my nerves acting up?

I'm here for the surf, okay? Not him. Never him. I slide a hand down my sleek wetsuit to feel the swimsuit underneath. *Focus, Violet, remember why you're here.*

Do I miss him? Hell yeah. Do I wish he would talk to me? Absolutely. But we both made our stand clear. I need to respect that. Let him be.

Here's the deal about surf competitions. They aren't always gender-separated. Not this one, anyway. Guys, gals, we're all out there together. Riding the same waves, facing the same rush. The sea doesn't discriminate, why should we?

But enough about that. I need to focus. This is my first competition and the last thing I need is to wipeout in front of all these people. *And him.*

He's probably here somewhere, acting all broody and aloof. Classic Ryan. I can almost see him, resting against his truck, surfboard beside him. Ugh, why does my mind do this?

I shake my head to clear the cobwebs. *Get it together, Vi. No time for Ryan-drama. Focus on the surf. The ride. That's why you're here.*

I take a deep breath and let it out slowly. The salty air fills my lungs, calms my racing heart. I can do this. I need to do this. For me.

And then I spot him. Cole. Just the sight of him, tanned and smirking like he owns the world, makes my blood boil. As if I didn't have enough on my plate already. Thanks universe, real classy.

I take a moment to regroup. Okay, deep breath, Vi. You've got this. He's just a guy, a guy your parents chose, but a guy, nonetheless.

Geez. Focus Vi! Focus.

Alright, let's get this show on the road. I'm sporting my favorite wetsuit and rocking the hell out of it, if I do say so myself.

The beach is packed. Kids making sandcastles, moms on the lookout, dads with cameras, everybody is in the spirit. And then there are the surfers. We're all just fish, ready to get back to the water.

The judges - they're in their highchairs, shielding their eyes against the sun. Clipboards in hand, looking serious. Surfing's no joke, after all. They've got that scrutinizing gaze down to a tee.

People have gathered around, some on beach towels, some with their feet digging into the sand, all eyes on the sea. The smell of saltwater is so strong I can taste it.

As for the surfers, we're all lined up like soldiers ready for battle. Wetsuits hugging our bodies, surfboards under our arms, eyes on the horizon, we all know what's at stake.

And then there's Ryan. I spot him from the corner of my eye. Looking all focused, probably contemplating the waves or something. He's not paying attention to me. Good. I don't need that kind of distraction.

Then, the horn. The sign to get going. No turning back now. It's go time. As I sprint towards the water, surfboard ready, I know this is where I'm meant to be.

Forget Ryan. Forget Cole. This is about me, the waves, and nothing else. Let's do this, Bailey.

The ocean is a different kind of battlefield. No rules here except to stay on your board, which is easier said than done when facing ten-foot walls of water.

Everyone's fighting for their own wave. It's a mad scramble. People are falling left and right, eaten up by the surf. Looks like the ocean's having surfers for breakfast today.

I keep my head in the game. I can't afford to fall now. I remember Ryan's words, like they're playing on a loop in my head. *"Paddle hard, stand quick, lean forward."*

The screaming crowd, the whistling wind, the constant buzzing in my ears. Everything quiets before I challenge the raw power of the sea.

A mountain of water is coming straight for me. My heart lurches. This is it. This wave, this mass of frothing white and deep, shadowy blue... it's mine. A rolling thunder that, for a brief moment, has my name written all over it.

Paddle. I force my arms to move, push the water behind me. The saltwater stings my eyes, my arms feel like lead. The wave is fast approaching. Like a predator closing in on its prey. There's no escape, no retreat. And there's no tomorrow if I don't catch this wave.

Suddenly, the ocean lifts. It feels like I'm being hoisted up by a gigantic hand, the world tilting beneath me. The wave has me. Now, it's ride or drown.

Push up. Stand. I'm up before I know it. My feet find purchase on the slippery board. I'm riding, carving a path on the liquid beast. Colors and sounds merge into an adrenaline-fueled haze. The cheers of the crowd sound like distant thunder. I'm doing it. I'm really doing it.

But it's far from over. As soon as one wave dies, another takes its place. Bigger, meaner, a foaming nightmare of epic proportions. My pulse quickens.

It's coming at me fast, a charging bull made of water and fury. But I'm not scared. Can't afford to be. Fear's a luxury I don't have right now.

Brace. I press my feet into the board, grip the sides. Lean forward. I'm ready. Ready to take on the ocean, the world, anything it throws my way.

And then, the unthinkable happens. That gigantic beast of a wave I'd sworn to conquer, it bites back. I'm thrown off balance, caught off guard. My board slips out from under me, and suddenly, I'm falling.

The world goes silent. Time slows. Everything feels so... weightless. Like I'm a feather suspended in mid-air. And then...the ocean swallows me. A mouthful of salt water, bitter and cold. It's like a slap in the face. A wake-up call. *I've screwed up. Big time.*

Swimming back up to the surface is a battle of wills. My chest feels like it's on fire. I need air, I need to breathe. And then I break the surface, gasping, coughing. I'm welcomed back into the world by the searing California sun and the distant hum of the crowd.

As I bob there in the water, I realize something. Ryan's still out there. He's on his board, looking my way. I can't see his face, but I don't need to. He was probably expecting this. Probably saw it coming from a mile away.

With a frustrated sigh, I swim back to the shore. Every stroke feels heavy, every breath harder to catch. I'm exhausted. Mentally, physically, emotionally... every part of me feels spent.

Reaching the sands, I half crawl, half stumble out of the water. My legs feel like jelly. Alec's there, handing me my towel. His eyes are full of sympathy, but it only makes my heart sink deeper.

"You did good, Vi," he says. A lie, coated with sugar.

"No, I didn't," I retort, wrapping the towel around me. "I screwed up. I fell. I... I lost."

But deep down, I know it's not about the fall, the loss, or the disappointment. It's about proving something to myself. And maybe, just maybe, to Ryan as well. That I can do this. That I'm not a lost cause.

I am drenched and shivering. I make a silent vow to myself. I'll make it right. For myself, for Ryan, for everyone who's ever believed in me. I'll ride that beast of a wave, conquer it. And next time, it won't be the ocean that comes out victorious.

It'll be me.

And then, out of nowhere, there it is. The Big Kahuna. The wave of all waves. A monster. It's brewing out there, ready to crash and roar and show us all who's boss.

And guess who's going for it? Yup, Ryan's out there, paddling fast, eyes on the prize. And... oh boy, Cole too.

24

FIGHTING FOR BREATH

RYAN

I'm paddling out, the sea feels like my second home. I feel the swell beneath me, growing, calling my name.

Cole's not far off. The prick thinks he's got it in the bag. He's looking over at me, that smug smile plastered on his pretty-boy face.

The sun's up, glinting off the water, and I can see a wave start to build. It's mine, I know it. I set my gaze, paddle hard, ignoring the burn in my shoulders.

It's a big one, a skyscraper of a wave, all foamy and raring to go. I push up, feet planted. Balance. Ride. That's the mantra. Cole's a speck in my periphery, but I don't give him a second glance.

The wave roars beneath me, I'm king of the world. I lean, make a sharp cut, spray flies. A cheer erupts from the beach. Suddenly, I see it. A wall of water building, even bigger than the one I'm on. A giant. The crowd on the shore gasps, I can hear it over the thunder of my wave.

It's not just a wave, it's a challenge. A mountain to conquer. It's like the ocean is daring us, Cole and me. We lock eyes, we both know it's coming.

To hell with Cole, I think, feeling the adrenaline surge. This is my wave. And I'm going to ride it.

There's no room for fear, only focus. I feel the wave swell behind me, feel its power. I can't afford to miss this. Not for anything.

I dig my fingers into the water and paddle like hell. I'm stealing this wave from Cole, no two ways about it. The wave towers over me, a moving skyscraper, all power and promise. I can feel it in my bones, feel it urging me on. Now's the moment.

Suddenly, there's a shadow. Cole. He's on the same wave. The audacity of the man. But this isn't a team sport, Cole.

We're side by side, racing down the beast. It's a fight to the finish, a battle of balance. Who'll wipe out, who'll ride it out, the crowd's holding its breath.

Then he does something unthinkable. He nudges my board. I nearly lose my balance. Sneaky bastard. But I regain it, I'm still riding. The war's not over yet.

I give him a glare that could curdle milk, but he just smirks. Well, two can play at this game. I wait for the perfect moment, then nudge him back.

For a moment, everything's in slow motion. Cole's eyes widen, he teeters, but he doesn't fall. We're still neck and neck, the beach is just a blurry line ahead.

We're defying gravity, physics, probably a couple of surfing regulations.

My foot slips, the balance goes south. *Well, shit!* I know what's coming. The crowd's gasp mirrors my own surprise.

For a moment, everything's a blur of water and sky. I'm going down, I know it. But then, something kicks in, some stubborn, grumpy, die-hard part of me.

I grit my teeth, muscles straining, arms flailing. I claw my way back, fight gravity, fight the fall. The board shakes, quivers, then steadies.

I blink away the saltwater, find myself still upright. I breathe. The crowd roars. I'm back in the game.

I look around, find Cole. His eyes are wide, stunned. His smirk's wiped off, replaced with something like respect.

A wave of victory washes over me. I can taste it, feel it. But I keep my cool.

The ocean's pissed. The waves are evil, gnarly things. Cole's up next, right in the path of a wave that's angry as hell.

He tries to tackle it. Bad move. The wave's got a mind of its own and Cole's not on its good side.

The beast of a wave crashes. Cole's a goner, chewed up and spit out. His board does a little dance in the sky.

Damn. I never signed up for a horror show. I see him bob back up, a human cork. He's alive, and that's good enough for me.

I've won. But the victory beer's gonna taste a little sour. I glance at Cole, and then at the indifferent ocean. Life's a cruel teacher.

For a moment, I think about Cole. Not as the douche in the fancy suit, but as a bloke who just faced down a pissed-off ocean. Makes you think.

As I turn away from the water, the cheers hit me. I won, didn't I? Yeah, I did. But the win feels different. It's not just about me, it's about surviving the ocean's bad hair day.

But, hell, I've learned something today. And it's not just to avoid the ocean when she's on the warpath. It's about respect. Respect for the ocean, for the game, and yeah, even for Cole.

The cheers bring me back. This is my moment, my win. But I can't help but look at the water again. The ocean might've kicked our asses today, but we're still here. And that's worth more than any trophy.

Suddenly the cheers die down. There's this weird hush hanging over the crowd. Like when you hit pause on a movie. A sort of 'what the hell' moment.

I peer through the swarm of bodies. Brows knotted; lips pursed. Some pointing out towards the sea. I crane my neck, can't see shit.

Look, I may not be on the clock, but the lifeguard in me never takes a day off. If there's trouble, I'm there. It's a reflex. Like blinking. Or hating kale.

Muscling my way through the crowd, I elbow a path towards the beach. Sweat slick on my back, sand grinding between my toes. Frickin' circus, this place.

Everyone's huddled together like penguins in a snowstorm. They part like the Red Sea as I approach, their eyes wide, lips flapping with whispers.

I push through, heart thumping a little faster, a little harder. Something's off. The air's got a taste of dread, like biting into a bad apple.

Just a few more feet and I'm there. At the edge of the crowd, at the edge of the unknown. I'm not sure what to expect.

I worm my way through, a fish through coral. The people part, whispers follow me. "What happened?" I ask the closest face, but I get nothing back. Nada. Just wide eyes and open mouths.

The first thing that catches my eye is a swatch of green. A green that doesn't belong on the sand. Doesn't belong among the swirl of colors. It's a wetsuit. Violet's wetsuit.

My breath hitches.

Then the shock of red hair sprawled out, catching the sun's rays. The color of sunsets and ripe apples. That's not a color you forget. It's her. Violet.

The sight slams into me, stopping me dead in my tracks.

"Vi?" My voice is a ghost's whisper, an echo in the buzz of noise around me. She's not moving. Not stirring. Hell, she's as still as the grave.

Panic, that old unwelcome friend, punches me hard in the gut. My heart turns into a wild animal in my chest, trying to break free. I can hear the blood rush in my ears, deafening, drowning everything else.

Alec's there, hovering over her like a hawk, yelling her name. But she doesn't respond. Doesn't even twitch. I move, push past him without a second thought, fall to my knees next to her.

"Vi?" I reach out, my hand shaking, and touch her cheek. It's cold. Ice cold. And I realize I'm holding my breath.

Tossing and turning, thrashing around like a fish out of water. Guilt gnaws at my insides. I should have been there. Should have done something.

People are starting to gather, their curious eyes on us. Too many eyes. I want to tell them to piss off, but I can't find the words.

And then, just as the panic is about to take me under, the sirens blare. A lifeguard patrol vehicle is cutting through the crowd, racing towards us.

"Vi?" I call out to her again. Because I can't not. Because it's the only thing I can do right now. But she doesn't answer. She doesn't even blink. And my heart feels like it might shatter.

I'm on my feet before I know it, reaching out, lifting her. God, she feels so light. Too light. Like she's not there. Like she's just a shadow of the fiery, sassy redhead who gave me hell on the waves.

But she's here, in my arms, and I'm moving. Sand crunches under my feet, the world blurs around me. All I can see is the lifeguard vehicle pulling up. All I can hear is the pounding of my heart.

Alec is at my heels, stuttering something. A question or plea? I can't make it out. I can't think past the lump in my throat, the fear clawing its way up my spine.

"Let me come with you," he's saying. Demanding. His voice a high-pitched whine in the back of my head.

I shake my head. "Follow in your car." My voice is steel. No room for argument. Not now. Not with Violet like this.

"But-" he starts, and I cut him off with a look. A look that says shut up, a look that says back off.

"Will she be okay?" His voice is small. Small and scared.

I don't know the answer. I don't have the words. So I give him the only thing I've got. A glare that could freeze hell over.

I shift Violet in my arms, feeling her weight against me. My heart skips a beat. I want to tell her to wake up, to fight, to be the tough-as-nails spitfire I know. But the words are stuck.

So I look at Alec, my eyes burning a hole through him, and I don't say a thing. Because right now, there are no words. Just the weight of a girl who should be laughing and fighting, not lying here like this.

With that, I turn away, step into the patrol vehicle, and shut the door. The world outside becomes a blur of sand and sun and faces I don't care about. All I can focus on is the redhead in my arms, her hair a halo of fire against the harsh white of the ambulance interior.

It's just me and her. The rest of the world can wait. It's got to.

25

AN AWAKENING

VIOLET

I hardly open my eyes to a sea of sterile white. Blinking, I try to figure out where I am. It doesn't take long to realize. Only one place in the world smells like disinfectant and despair.

A hospital.

What the hell happened?

Bits and pieces flutter through my brain. The competition, the heat, the waves. Did I...did I pass out? God, that's embarrassing.

Why, though? Not eating? Stress? Both? I wouldn't be surprised. After all, it's been a hell of a day. Weeks of hell. Time is a fuzzy concept right now.

And then there's a blurry memory. Arms around me, a steady voice. Who was that?

I scrunch up my face, trying to piece it together. The voice. ..familiar, but gruff. Was it Alec?

A frown creases my forehead. Please, not Cole. Anyone but Cole.

I push the thought aside, the idea of his smug face looming over me just too much to handle right now. Instead, I focus on my breathing. In, out. Slow, steady.

Just like riding a wave.

In a weak attempt at regaining some dignity, I try to sit up. I'm grimacing as the room sways. Okay, maybe not. Lying down it is.

A groan slips out before I can stop it. I'm the one who always stays upright, who always stays strong. But right now, I'm as flimsy as a wet noodle.

Fine, Violet. Lay low. For now.

But whoever dragged me into this hospital had bed better watch out. Because once I'm up, there will be hell to pay.

Slowly, I open my eyes, blinking away the sterile brightness of the room. The world outside is blurry.

What time is it? Late, I'm guessing. Or maybe early.

Hospitals really know how to screw with your internal clock.

Then, I feel it. A warmth wrapped around my hand, too solid to be a blanket. I shift my gaze. It's a hand. A big, tan hand. Holding mine.

Blinking, I follow the hand up to an arm. The arm is attached to a sleeping figure in the visitor's chair which is pulled close to the bed. Light hair, tanned skin, familiar shirt. The puzzle pieces click together.

Ryan.

My breath hitches. It's Ryan. Mr. Lifeguard, Mr. Surfer Dude. Why the hell is he here?

More importantly, why is he holding my hand?

I glance at our entwined fingers, mine pale against his. There's something strange, something oddly comforting about the sight. I'm not sure I like it.

Okay, I might like it a little.

He's asleep, slouched in the chair, his face uncharacteristically relaxed. His blonde hair falls over his eyes, softening his features. He's not so bad, I guess. When he's unconscious.

I wonder how long he's been here. He looks exhausted. The dark circles under his eyes could be a testament to a hard night's surfing. Or perhaps, a sleepless night at my bedside?

Which is weird. Super weird.

Did he carry me here? The memory is hazy, but I think... I think it was him. I remember his voice. A steady anchor in the whirlwind of chaos. The idea sends a strange shiver down my spine.

But why? We're not friends, not anymore really. Competitors. Lifeguard-swimmer, sure. But him being here, holding my hand in a hospital room... that's a different story.

I could wake him, I suppose. Get some answers. But instead, I find myself watching him sleep, his chest rising and falling in the dim light. A strange calm settles over me. It's... nice.

God, I must be more messed up than I thought.

But still, I don't pull my hand away. Instead, I squeeze his hand lightly. I watch as he stirs, murmuring something unintelligible in his sleep.

The room is still quiet when Ryan stirs. It's like I've somehow cued him with my thoughts. How's that for a talent? He jerks awake, eyes blinking open to meet mine.

That's different. Usually, his gaze has this way of sliding past me or avoiding me. But now, his focus is solely on me. Me in my hospital bed, sporting my oh-so-fashionable gown. And apparently holding his hand.

He jolts, pulling his hand back as if he's touched a hot stove. My warm, secure feeling evaporates, and I fight back a wave of, I don't know, disappointment? That can't be right. I am wearing a ring on that hand anyway.

"You good?" His voice is gruff, still rough with sleep. It sounds like he gargles with pebbles for breakfast.

"Yeah," I reply, a bit too fast. "I'm fine. Where's Alec? My parents?" *I deliberately do not name Cole, my supposed husband to be.*

"They're on the way. Alec went to get them." His eyes dart to the side, looking anywhere but at me.

His admission triggers another jumbled memory. "Did you ... carry me here?" I ask, my voice smaller than I'd like.

"Yeah," he mumbles, not meeting my gaze. I should say thanks, I suppose. But the words stick in my throat.

"Did I pass out?" I say instead.

He nods, rubbing the back of his neck. "They think it's dehydration. Tests should be here soon."

I feel a weird mix of relief and embarrassment. Dehydration? Seriously? What am I, an amateur?

With a sigh, I push myself up, resting on my elbows. The world tilts a little, but I grit my teeth and sit up.

Ryan is on his feet in an instant, hovering near me like a nervous pigeon. "Take it easy," he warns. His eyes are wide and worried. His look is unnerving.

I scoff, more to convince myself than him. "I'm fine, Ryder. Just a little thirsty, is all."

His lips twitch into a small smile. It's a rare sight, like spotting a unicorn in the wild. He shakes his head, crossing his arms over his chest.

"Well, next time remember to hydrate," he grumbles, sinking back into his chair.

I roll my eyes, settling back against the pillows. "Thanks for the advice, Lifeguard."

His chuckle is soft, lost in the quiet hum of the hospital. But I hear it. And despite everything, I smile.

Maybe having Ryan around isn't so bad. I feel comfortable. Comforted.

"Well, next time," I grumble, mimicking his gruff voice, "remember not to fall asleep in a chair. You'll get a crick in your neck."

Ryan huffs, rubbing his neck subconsciously. His eyes narrow, the corners crinkling. "Did anyone ever tell you you're annoying when you're ill?"

"I aim to please," I reply, delivering my best innocent smile. He gives me a pointed look, but there's a hint of a smile in there somewhere.

We lapse into silence. It's not the awkward, suffocating kind. It's more of a comfortable quiet, the kind that doesn't demand words. It feels nice.

Then Ryan breaks it. "You scared us, Vi. You really did." His voice is lower, softer, stripped of the usual sarcasm.

"I didn't mean to," I say, my voice barely a whisper.

He sighs, rubbing his hand over his face. "I know."

Another stretch of silence. It's different this time. It's the kind that holds words we're not saying. Words that are too heavy, too real for our usual banter.

"I appreciate you being here," I whisper softly and truthfully.

Ryan's brows furrow, he looks almost vulnerable. "I couldn't leave you alone," he mumbles in a confessional sort of way.

The moment hangs heavy, and then it's gone, shattered when Ryan snorts and shakes his head. "Just don't make a habit of it. I've got better things to do than play nurse."

"I'll do my best," I assure him, grinning.

"Good," he replies, shooting me a mock-stern look. But his eyes are softer, warmer. It's a side of him I haven't seen before.

And I like it.

It's a surprising thought, one that leaves me reeling. But then Ryan laughs, breaking the tension. He pulls me back into the comfortable rhythm we've found. And just like that, things feel normal again.

"So... you heard about the engagement, huh?" My words hang in the air, a neon sign blinking between us. His reaction is instant.

26

TWO PEAS IN A POD

VIOLET

I watch as Ryan tenses, avoids my gaze, his eyes darting around the sterile room. His lips press into a tight line. "Can we not talk about that?" he grumbles, the usual sassy edge in his voice replaced with something raw.

"Nope," I say, popping the 'p'. "It's about time we did."

His Adam's apple bobs as he swallows, his eyes still refusing to meet mine.

The engagement. It was a grenade and I'd just pulled the pin.

"Ryan," I begin, my voice softer this time. "I had to."

He's quiet for a moment. Then, "Had to what, Vi?"

"I had to say yes." The words taste sour as they tumble out.

"Why?" It's not angry or bitter. It's genuine curiosity. A question he's been carrying around.

I take a deep breath. "Because... because it's what was expected of me."

He snorts. "Since when does Violet Bailey care about what's expected of her?"

"Since I realized I could hurt people if I didn't." The truth of the words rings between us.

He stiffens, his eyes finally meeting mine. They're a storm of emotions I can't decipher.

"We didn't talk for weeks, Ry," I continue. "I thought I'd lost you."

Something flickers in his eyes. "You thought you'd lost me *after* you got engaged to another man?" His words are thick with sarcasm and bitterness.

I flinch. When he puts it like that, it sounds awful.

"Ry..."

"No, Vi," he interrupts. His voice is tight, but his gaze never wavers. "I get it."

"You do?" I ask, hope flaring in my chest.

"No," he replies, but his hand is back on mine, his touch soothing the stinging hurt his words left. "But I will."

Ryan releases my hand and pushes himself off the chair. There's a sudden chill in the absence of his touch. "I should probably get going," he mumbles, shuffling towards the door. "Your parents aren't exactly my fan club and they should be here any minute."

"And I don't want your fiancé to get jealous," he adds, a shadow of his old smirk dancing on his lips. A pang of something I can't name hits me square in the chest.

The grimace on my face is my only reply.

There's a lump in my throat, one I can't swallow.

I clear my throat. "You looked great at the competition today, Ry." The words hang in the silence, a compliment wrapped in a plea.

He stops, his hand resting on the doorknob. His smile is soft when he turns back to me. "Thanks, Vi. So did you."

"No," I shake my head, pulling the hospital blanket closer around me. "I messed up, Ryan. Big time."

His eyebrows furrow, as if he's trying to solve a particularly tough puzzle. "No," he counters. "I saw you catch that first wave. It was a big one, Vi."

I can feel my cheeks heating up. "You... you watched?"

He shrugs, but there's a glint in his eyes I can't quite read. "Yes. And you did good."

The heat in my cheeks spreads through me, warmth curling in my stomach. Ryan watched me surf. Despite everything, he watched.

And suddenly, the hospital room doesn't feel so cold anymore.

Ryan is about to make his grand exit, one hand on the door, when he pauses. He turns, his eyes soft. "Make sure to get a lot of rest, alright?" His voice is more tender than I remember.

An ocean of emotions spin inside me. "And drink water," he adds, a sheepish grin tugging at the corners of his lips. That brings a genuine chuckle out of me.

"Yes, sir," I respond, my voice not as steady as I'd like. I don't want him to go. Not yet. I feel like we're so close to something. It's something that feels dangerously like a breakthrough.

He nods, that familiar smirk back in place. "Good." And then he's turning to leave, the moment slipping away.

Before he can leave, the door swings open. A nurse, cheery and a little too bright for my taste, breezes in.

"Nice that I caught you both," she chirps, clipboard clutched in her hand. I blink at her, the sudden shift too jarring, while Ryan freezes in the doorway. For once, I'm glad for the interruption.

Maybe I'm not ready for that breakthrough just yet. Maybe I need a little more time. After all, time heals, right? That's what they say. But then again, they also say drink lots of water.

I chuckle to myself, letting the nurse's incessant chatter wash over me. Whatever is happening between Ryan and me can wait. At least for now.

The nurse's entrance breaks the tension in the room. Ryan, caught in the doorway, offers a tight-lipped smile, quickly retreating to sit by the wall. He's silent, watching.

I note the hardness in his eyes, a shell protecting a hint of worry. He is the same gruff, unyielding Ryan, but with a softness peeking through. I tuck the observation away, saving it for later dissection.

The nurse, a ball of energy wrapped in scrubs, is full of chatter. I glance at her badge. "Molly," it reads. She rattles off medical terms like she's reciting her grocery list - so ordinary, so practiced.

Molly retrieves a folder, beaming at us. "I've got your test results here, Miss..."

"Bailey," I supply, my throat parched. "Violet Bailey."

Ryan stands across the room, staring at his shoes. His usual sturdy demeanor seems a bit shaken. Is he nervous? I guess we're two peas in a pod.

Molly nods, flipping open the folder. Her eyes flit over the page, then flicker between me and Ryan. She beams, assuming, "You must be Mr. Bailey then."

My breath catches. Ryan's face turns an adorable shade of red, and I almost laugh. He's got that deer-in-the-headlights look, surprised and cornered.

Her assumption lays thick in the room. We let it simmer, neither of us offering a correction. Is it the shock? Or is it the acceptance of a reality that isn't ours but feels strangely comfortable?

And there it is. A smirk pulls at my lips. The idea of Ryan, as "Mr. Bailey" is absurd, but strangely compelling.

Molly then pulls out the punchline, disguised in her chirpy voice. "Well, congratulations, you two!" A pause. "You're expecting."

The room spins, the world tilts on its axis. I feel myself swallow; the taste of hospital sterility strong in my throat.

Shock. Pure, unadulterated shock. The kind that sends your head buzzing, your heart pounding. You think you're prepared for the storm, then the thunder hits.

Ryan shifts in his seat. His face turns whiter than the walls around us. He looks as if he's seen a ghost.

"What?!" The words tumble from my lips before I can even think. "Are you sure?"

Molly's face softens. "Oh boy, I guess this wasn't planned?"

"No, definitely not..." My voice trails off. I don't even know what I'm trying to say. My head's a whirl of thoughts, spinning faster than I can grasp.

Ryan shifts uncomfortably. His voice is unusually soft, his usual cockiness replaced by uncertainty. "We didn't... I mean, we weren't..."

Molly's sympathetic smile is the last thing I see before my eyes close. I take a deep breath, letting reality sink in. *A baby.*

My eyes are still closed when I hear my brother's voice in the doorway.

27

ON LOVE'S LOST SHORES

RYAN

I never thought I'd be in my parents' kitchen at this hour, under these circumstances. Their faces, usually soft and warm, are stern now. I guess it's hard to smile when your son drops a baby bombshell in the middle of the night.

"Ryan, this is a serious matter," my dad says, running a hand through his salt-and-pepper hair.

No kidding, Sherlock.

"It's not like I planned this, Dad." My voice is strained. I'm desperately trying to keep it together. For Vi. For the baby.

My mom just stands there, clutching her hands in disbelief. She's got this way of making silence deafening.

I rub my forehead, trying to push back the impending headache. I didn't come here for an interrogation. *I need support. I need allies.*

"I know I messed up, but I need your help." I feel like a teenager again, admitting to sneaking out for a midnight surf.

Dad stares at me for a long moment. I see a flicker of sympathy in his eyes. Or maybe it's just the low kitchen light playing tricks.

"Are you sure the baby is yours?" Mom spits out. I choke on my coffee. I wasn't ready for that. But then again, when am I ever ready with them?

My parents don't like Violet or the Baileys. They made that clear years ago. But this, this is a new low.

"Yes, Mom. Pretty damn sure," I snap back. Cool it, Ryan. This isn't the time to lose your temper. These are your parents. *Breathe.*

"You were always reckless, Ryan. Always running headfirst into trouble," Dad grumbles, shaking his paper. I roll my eyes. Not this talk again.

The tension in the room could snap a steel wire. I get it. I do. They're worried. I'm worried. But this isn't about them. It's about Vi. It's about our baby.

"Look, this isn't what I planned either," I repeat, softer now. "But it's happening. It's real. And I won't let you or anyone else cast doubts on this."

Mom and Dad look at each other. Silent conversation. *I hate it when they do that.*

Finally, Dad looks at me, grumbles something under his breath. Mom's lips are pressed into a thin line. She nods, but there's no warmth in her eyes. It's clear. This isn't over.

"If you think we're going to support this, you're wrong."

I turn around and lean against the door frame. *Keep cool, Ryan.* "What's that supposed to mean?"

Dad stands, hands on the table. His voice, icy as winter, says, "Your inheritance, Ryan. Consider it gone if you pursue this."

A laugh slips out before I can stop it. Inheritance. Of course, they would bring up money. I cross my arms, square my shoulders. "I don't need your money, Dad."

"It's not just about the money, son." Mom's voice cuts in, quieter, but just as sharp. "You're ruining your future."

I shake my head, stifle a groan. "Vi and the baby are my future."

Shock washes over both their faces. Good. Dad's mouth opens and closes, a fish on dry land. Mom's shaking her head, disbelief coloring her features.

"You don't understand, Ryan," Dad starts again. His grip on the back of his chair is white-knuckled.

"No, *you* don't understand." I cut him off. "I love her. I love our baby. And no inheritance, no threat, no damn judgement is going to change that."

"Ryan," Mom pleads.

"I have made my choice." I push off the door frame, stand tall. Stand firm. "And I'm sticking to it."

I see them exchange glances, and I don't wait for a response. I've said what I needed to. The ball is in their court now.

I walk out of the room, leaving behind a stunned silence. Their voices follow me out, but I don't turn back. *Don't look back. Move forward, wherever that leads.*

The house now feels like a prison. The walls seem to be closing in. I need to get out. *Air. Space. The beach.* I snatch my keys from the hall table, swing the front door open, and I'm out.

The drive is a blur. I can't shake their words out of my head. The sting, though, it's not as bad as I thought. Instead, there's a weird sense of liberation as if I'm breathing for the first time.

Sand crunches beneath my shoes as I step onto the beach. It's empty. Just me and the endless ocean. I plop down, draw my knees to my chest. *Damn, it's colder than I thought.*

I take out my phone. Her name shines back at me from the screen. Vi. I click on it, start a new message.

*I could use some company.
Beach. No pressure.*

I hit send before I can talk myself out of it. She might not come. She might be busy.

I shove the phone back into my pocket, push the thoughts away. *She'll come if she can. I know her.* The ocean's rhythmic whispers become my lullaby. The beach, our beach, has always been my escape, my hideaway. Now, it's my solace.

I lie back on the sand, hands tucked behind my head. Above me, the dark night sky is a canvas, splashed with an infinity of stars. Watching and breathing, my mind drifts to happier times. The times when it was just Vi and me, no complications, no consequences.

A bitter smile pulls at my lips. Kids. *Hell, we're about to have one*. Still, I can't help but wonder if I'm ready for this. For the late nights and the diaper changes. The first words and steps. The tantrums and the responsibilities. But then I remember, it's Vi. It's us. We've handled bigger waves. Pun intended.

I'm drawn out of my thoughts by the soft ping of my phone. I glance at the screen. A message from Vi.

On my way.

Damn, she's really coming.

I push myself up, dust off some sand. As I wait, I watch the waves crash onto the shore. The power, the raw energy, is humbling. The ocean is like life, throwing curveballs, trying to knock me down. *But I keep pushing. Keep moving. No matter what.*

In the dim light of the moon, a familiar figure appears in the distance. I stand, dusting the sand off my pants. She's here. She's really here. And suddenly, everything feels a little less overwhelming. A little more manageable.

Her figure becomes clearer as she walks closer. I can't help it. I move towards her.

I open my arms, intending to wrap her in a warm embrace, to find the comfort we both need. But something's off. Vi barely responds. It's like hugging a mannequin.

"Are you okay... Vi?" I ask, pulling back to look at her face. I study her for a moment. Her eyes, usually sparkling with mischief, look dull.

"I don't know, Ry,"

She hugs herself, as if trying to keep herself together. It hurts, seeing her like this. I want to fix it, fix everything, but I don't know how.

I kick at the sand, watching the grains scatter in the wind. "Vi," I start, "you know I care about you, right?"

There's a pause, her face unreadable in the moonlight. "Do you, Ry?"

The sharpness in her voice stings. "Of course, I do."

She huffs, crossing her arms. "That's the problem, isn't it?"

I furrow my brow. "How's that a problem?"

Her next words come out in a rush, a torrent of hurt and fear. "My parents, they... they don't want the baby."

A cold fear washes over me. "What? But why?"

"They think it'll ruin my life. That it'll ruin... us."

"Us?" I can't help but hope. "You're breaking up with Cole?"

"They insist I marry him, Ry." Her voice cracks, the silence stretching between us echoing her despair.

"But... but the baby..." My voice is a mere whisper now, carried away by the sea breeze.

Her response leaves me reeling. "I... I can't have it, Ry."

The world comes to a standstill. "You... what?"

"I... I have to get rid of it." Her words, though spoken quietly, explode in my ears like a bomb. The aftershock leaves me numb, my mind spinning, adrenalin rushing, heart pounding.

"But... Vi..." I'm at a loss for words. This is a possibility I never considered, a true shock. *A swift punch to the gut.* This is not what I expected. This is not what I want.

"Ry, I... I don't have a choice."

"Vi, there has to be another way..."

She shakes her head, stepping back. "It's not that simple, Ry."

"But, you... we..." I stumble over my words, grasping for something, anything.

"We...?" she prompts, the question hanging heavy in the air.

"We could... fight this together." I blurt out, desperation flooding my voice. "We could... we could be a family."

She takes another step back. "Ry, you don't understand."

"Then explain it to me, Miss Bailey."

Her voice breaks, the pain clear in her eyes. "You have your own life. I can't drag you into my messy soap opera."

"But I want to be dragged in."

"No, you don't, Ry." She sighs, glancing away. "Not like this."

"I don't care how it is, Vi. I care about you."

She looks at me, the pain in her eyes piercing my heart. "That's why I can't, Ry."

"Can't what?"

"I can't let you throw your life away because I'm pregnant."

She turns to leave, and it feels like the ground is giving way beneath my feet. "Vi..."

"I'm sorry, Ry." Her voice is quiet, carrying the weight of our world as she walks away. She leaves me standing alone on the beach, the waves crashing and the wind howling.

28

NO KNIGHT IN SIGHT

VIOLET

The silence in the townhouse is deafening. Maybe it's the guilt or just my growling stomach, reminding me of the skipped meals. Every time I glance at my reflection, it screams back, showing the toll of the last few weeks. The more weight I drop, the more I stress about the little life inside of me.

I'm back in Torrance without Alissa and without the bustle of our teaching lives. It leaves me hollow. Looking at the line of photos on the wall, I see the two of us moving in, on the first day of school. And then there's the gang on the beach last summer, all smiles. *Wow. Alec looks much younger.*

My breath catches when I see Ryan and me, in a group, all smiles.

Funny how things change. Our laughter from that day feels like a different lifetime.

Absent from the pictures, of course, is Cole. Always out of the frame, off to the side, looking in but never belonging.

Funny how some things change, but some things don't.

I clutch my stomach, sending a silent apology to the little one. An unexpected tear drops. Note to self: when did I get so damn emotional?

All those rom-coms I've watched should have prepared me for this. Breakups, betrayals, and now babies. *My life is a bad Netflix series*.

In my head, I replay our beach talk, Ryan trying to reassure me, offering his support. But can he? My family won't let it happen. Cole is their solution to everything.

Cole is everything they want for me, and for themselves, but nothing I want. I never imagined being with anyone but Ryan. Yet here I am, choosing between my family's wishes and my own heart.

The baby. The one they want me to forget. I feel another stab of guilt. Maybe if I was stronger, braver, things would be different. But I can't change the past. I can only hope for a brighter tomorrow.

Knock, knock. Not now, universe. *Alec.*

"Vi, are okay in there?"

No, I'm not. Obviously. I open the door to my disheveled brother.

"Yes, I'm just gathering my thoughts."

"Looks more like they're scattering," he teases. Always the funny guy. If only he knew.

He drops into a chair and looks around. "You look... rough."

Oh, thanks. "Gee, you really know how to lift a girl's spirits."

He doesn't answer and gives me the look.

"What?" I snap.

He sighs, long and loud. "It's about the baby, isn't it?"

Bingo. "It's my baby, Alec."

Alec frowns, looking anywhere but at me. "It's not just your life on the line."

Low blow. "Whose side are you on?"

His face is grim. "Mom and Dad think it's best—"

I cut him off. "It's not their choice!"

He's clearly uncomfortable. "Vi, they want what's best for you. And, you know, there's still Cole."

Oh, please. "So, you're saying I should just forget Ryan and marry Cole? Be a good little girl and do as I'm told?"

Alec shifts uneasily. "It's complicated."

I can feel the anger bubbling. "I want this baby, Alec."

He doesn't meet my eyes. "Sometimes, what we want isn't what's best."

I stand up, feeling a rage I've never felt before. "So, I should just give up my child for family honor?"

Alec sighs again. "It's not that simple."

Yes, it is. "I thought you'd understand. Be on my side."

He moves closer, trying to bridge the gap. "I'm always on your side, Vi. Always. But you need to think about this, about Cole, about the future."

I move away. "I am thinking. Clearly more than you are."

He looks wounded. But that's not my problem right now. "Whatever you decide, just know I'm here."

Oh, sure. "Thanks, but I don't need more complications."

He stands, hands in his pockets. "Heard from Ryan lately?"

I raise an eyebrow. "Why would I?"

He shrugs. "Just asking."

Oh, come on. "Cut the crap, Alec." I take a deep breath. "Fine. I saw him. At the beach." My heart does this weird little flop.

He hesitates. "And?"

Well, that's just perfect. "I broke up with him."

His surprise turns to confusion. "Because of the baby?"

Partly. "Because of you guys."

Alec rubs the back of his neck. "Turns out, he's left town."

The breath leaves my chest and I whirl on Alec. "He what?"

Alec looks genuinely sympathetic. "He said he needed some time."

I sink back on the sofa. "Damn."

There's an awkward silence.

He finally says, "Maybe it's for the best." Alec is looking at his shoes, avoiding me.

Is it though? "Who the hell knows?"

133

Alec looks at me, searching. "You still love him." My brother is searching my face now, looking intently for a response to his statement.

I look away. "Does it matter?"

He sighs. "Everything's such a mess."

You're telling me. "Welcome to my world."

He cracks a half-smile. "Always so dramatic."

I stop the smile I feel forming and try to stare hard at him. "It's a gift."

Alec shakes his head, chuckling. "Never change, Sis."

I smirk. "I wouldn't dream of it."

Alec makes his exit, sort of slinking out more than walking, and I'm left in a suffocating silence. Funny how the emptiness seems louder now.

I fall back into the sofa and let my brother's words bounce around my head. Ryan's gone? Just like that? I hug a pillow, holding on like it's some kind of lifeline or a pathetic shield against my crumbling world.

Why is love so damn complicated? I mean, fairytales really sold us a load of crap.

A sting builds behind my eyes. I'm not crying. Nope. But my lashes have other plans, betraying me by getting all damp.

I can't even blame hormones for this.

The room blurs as one traitorous tear escapes, and then another. *Fuck.* The dam is broken now, and I've lost the plot.

I know I made the choice to protect Ryan to spare him from my family's drama. But did I think it through? Did I just mess up the best thing that ever happened to me?

A choked laugh slips out. *Seriously, Vi? Melodramatic much?*

But there's no escaping this heavy weight on my chest. All I can think is: Did I make a colossal mistake?

Okay. Deep breath, Vi.

The television drones on in the background. Some overly cheerful woman is hawking a mop. It's supposed to change my life. Right now, nothing short of a time machine can do that.

I've been sent here to end the pregnancy. But there's this little voice, that annoying inner-Vi, prodding at my insides. The reality of the clinic visit looms, casting a shadow over everything. Is it so bad to wish for a different reality?

My family is taking away my choice.

I glance at a family photo. There's me, beaming, sandwiched between two of the most controlling humans ever. "*It's not your body,*" I whisper to their frozen smiles.

Tears prick again. Ugh. I mentally slap them back.

My mind drifts, envisioning a child with dirty blonde hair, eyes with the mischief I fell for. Would she be the perfect blend of Ryan and me? Cheeky, smart, ridiculously good-looking? Obviously.

What if Ryan never comes back? What if I become the person my parents want, not the one I see in the mirror?

I'm brought back by the TV switching to a cartoon. A little character's running around, hair wild and golden. Maybe it's silly to see signs in a children's show. But damn it, life, why play with my emotions like this?

I chuckle, despite it all. Life's one crazy rollercoaster. And I didn't even buy a ticket.

Oh, come on, Violet. You've been through worse. You survived that horrid mushroom haircut in third grade, didn't you? I try a laugh, but it ends as a weak snort. There's a gaping Ryan-shaped hole in my evening, and no amount of self-deprecating humor can patch it up.

I lounge on the couch, tossing the remote from hand to hand. Every channel seems to scream 'romance'. A couple sharing an umbrella. Some oldies dancing in their living room. A freaking dog and cat nuzzling each other. Seriously? Nature's turning on me now?

By midnight, my phone's screen is smudged with fingerprints. Pictures of us, texts, stupid memes we shared. "*You ruined memes for me, Ryan,*" I tell the screen. It doesn't respond. Good, I'm not in the mood for Siri's sass.

My bed feels vast and cold. I curl up, surrounding myself with pillows, as if they could replace his warmth. The wind chimes ring, and I wonder if it's him, whispering from afar.

Closing my eyes, I allow myself a moment. A moment to miss him, to feel, to let go.

29

CALIFORNIA DREAMING

VIOLET

Ryan's image pops into my head, uninvited but not unwelcome. Ugh, why is my brain such a traitor?

The beach becomes vivid around me. Sand in places it shouldn't be, waves teasing my toes, that sunset that's to die for. But the main attraction is Ryan. That man, standing there like a Greek god ad for suntan lotion, all bronzed and glorious.

Look at him. Standing so confidently, his smile as tempting as sin. The same beach where dreams blossomed and then got squashed. He looks delicious with that sun-kissed skin. And those tell-tale summer freckles dotting his nose and cheeks. Pfft, who gave him the right?

Our gazes lock. An electric charge. He doesn't even need to speak. Those eyes, darting with hints of playfulness and... wait a minute, is that a dash of regret?

I'm dwarfed by him, as always. Petite Violet meets Tall, Tan, and Handsome. He strides closer, every step calculated, every move dripping with intention.

His lips. Oh, those lips. They're moving towards mine and my heart's trying to win some sort of Olympic sprint event.

There are no words, just that look. That look which says a thousand things and one very specific thing: "I've missed this."

His hands, warm and large, frame my face. Gentle yet firm. That kiss? It's like the first taste of ice cream on a scorching day. Familiar, but always, always so damn exhilarating.

It's a bit bold, but his tongue finds mine, like it's searching for a lost treasure. Geez, Ryan's oral navigation skills are out of this world.

"Ryan..." The name escapes, a whispered plea between breaths. Oh boy, does he have his hook in me. It's like my brain's taken a vacation and left my body in charge.

The little smirk playing on his lips says he heard me. "Yes?" Pulling back, those piercing eyes of his bore into mine, like he's looking for answers. Answers to questions I'm too flustered to even think of.

My fingers travel up, almost of their own accord, tracing the contours of his cheek. His eyelids flutter shut, lashes casting shadows on his tanned skin. Such a big guy but so darn cute in this moment.

His fingers intertwine with mine, grounding me, as the world seems to tilt. Oh, that smile. So tender, like he's holding a secret.

"I've missed you." Barely there, the confession brushes my ear.

"And here I thought it was just me," I breathe out. So, this is what being on cloud nine feels like.

Funny thing, this beach. Usually, it's bustling with noisy tourists and ice cream vendors. And overenthusiastic kids building sandcastles. Now? It's like someone waved a magic wand and gave us our own secluded paradise. Lucky us.

But before I can soak in the serenity, his lips crash onto mine once more. A slow burn, then a fiery explosion.

The weight of his palms on my waist has me short of breath. Okay, universe, I wasn't prepared for that! In my two-piece swimsuit, there's hardly anything left to the imagination. Suddenly, I'm hyper-aware of every inch of fabric. The sun, which usually cooks me like a lobster, now feels like a gentle caress. It's taking the backseat to the real heat right in front of me.

Oh, and speaking of heat! His lips are on my neck. The sensation is electrifying, tingles spreading everywhere. His body, taut and firm, draws me in. Hello there, Mr. Chiseled Chest meeting my... well, clearly excited bosom.

Really, hormones? Now? But there's no denying that rush. The reaction is primal. My nipples get hard when they get pressed to his chest.

"Ryan..." I mutter, because well, beach. Daytime. And scandal. "Someone's going to see us."

His response, muffled against my skin, is a simple, "Let them."

His wandering hands, oh those sneaky things, inch upwards. They venture under the thin fabric of my bikini top, cupping my breast.

It's as if every nerve ending in my body decided to have a little party. And, of course, my vocal cords make an appearance. Sounding out with a rather uncharacteristic, but utterly genuine moan. Thanks, body.

Suddenly, gravity isn't my friend anymore. Before I can compute, I'm on a sunbed of sand with Mr. Tall, Tan, and Terrific above me.

One moment my bikini is playing its very important role, and the next, with a crafty little move from him, it's off duty. Wait, did it just...? Yep. It did. Sun's out, buns out I guess.

Oh lord, there's that name again, spilling out of my lips. "Ryan..."

There's a trail of heat as his mouth ventures downwards. First, there's the delicate attention to my boobs. Oh boy, multitasking much? Licking and sucking on my one nipple while twisting the other one with his big hands.

But he doesn't stop. No, sir. The journey continues, mapping out every inch of my stomach. A pit stop at my belly button. Then, oh... the thighs.

This man and his mouth have a master plan. Each kiss to my inner thighs should come with a warning label. Because, honestly, who gave him the right?

Forget about diving into the sea. At this rate, I'm about to make my very own ocean right here.

Before I even get a chance to react, my bikini bottom meets its untimely demise. And suddenly, his mouth is right on my clit.

A push of encouragement from yours truly. Mmhm, he's getting all the feedback he needs. Then, there's that saucy addition of a finger. Followed by another. Boy, knows his math. The pleasure climbs, it's intoxicating, overwhelming, and I'm teetering right on the edge.

Then, life's biggest plot twist. My alarm. Just like that, from ecstasy to ear-piercing beeping.

6 AM on the dot. Talk about cruel timing! Why, alarm clock? Why today? Why now? Ugh. I can't lie here and spiral. The alarm was set for an early appointment, but as I pull on my faithful blue dress, I know I won't be driving to the clinic. I won't do it.

In the car, I turn on the radio softly and begin the drive to Malibu. I'm going back home to face whatever music the universe is preparing for me.

When I stop the car in front of the family mansion, the air outside is cool, just a touch of sun peeking out. Birds chirp their morning songs, and honestly, they sound as if they had a better night than I did. Show-offs.

I wrap my jacket tighter, taking in the neighborhood. Mrs. Watson is out watering her daisies. The cat from number 16 is giving me that judgmental stare. Note to self: It's high time I get a cat.

Reaching my front steps, there it is. Big. Bold. Red letters on an ugly yellow paper. "EVICTION NOTICE". For a moment, it's as if the world's pulled one over on Violet. Haha, very funny, Universe. I touch the paper, half hoping it's some twisted prank.

But no. There it is. The dirty deeds. One week. Unpaid taxes. "You've got to be kidding me."

As if life isn't enough of a rollercoaster, I think back to Dad. With his big dreams and bigger bets, always the promise of "one big win." But it seems luck ran out on us. Way out.

It all starts to click. Cole, with his too-shiny shoes and sleazy charm. Of course, he'd be the savior. Pay off our debts, give us a roof over our heads, all in exchange for yours truly.

Perfect. What's one more thing to trade, right? Add a wife to the list, along with those gold watches Dad pawned last month, and the circle is complete.

I let out a huff, head thumping against the door. I should have seen it coming. But then, when have I ever been great at predicting disasters?

I could break down. Cry. Let it all out. Or I could — what does Mom say? — pull myself up by my bootstraps. Do something. Anything. Before I'm out on the streets, and Mrs. Watson offers me a tent in her garden. Not today, Universe. Not today.

30

Unwritten Invitations

***

RYAN

The weight of the keys in my hand feels foreign, like they're to someone else's life. I've just stepped into a fancy, modern apartment I barely recognize. New town, new digs.

Who am I kidding? The lavish leather couch? Ordered online. The high-end kitchen gadgets? Also online. The windows offer a panorama of the city's skyline, but all I can see is the shadow of what I left behind.

My pocket vibrates, interrupting my thoughts. Pulling out the sleek new phone - latest model, naturally - I note the lack of smudged fingerprints. No history. No memories attached. A clean slate.

I swipe through the setup, and there's no "Violet" popping up with sassy texts. God, that woman. Could make me laugh when I was in my foulest mood. Right now? Probably lighting up someone else's phone with her jokes.

I sink onto the couch, the cool leather reminding me of the seats in my old office. Old life. Hell, everything's 'old' now. While staring at the bare walls, it dawns on me that I need to hang pictures. Do I even have any?

Alright, billionaire problems, I guess. Many people would kill for this kind of fresh start. New identity. New opportunities. But damn, is it lonely.

I look down at my attire. Same jeans, white tee, the uniform of a man who has too much but feels like he has too little. I need to shop, apparently. But who cares about brands when the threads of your past are frayed?

The doorbell rings. Speak of the devil. It's the delivery guy, some kid with headphones in, bobbing his head to a silent beat. Handing over the multiple bags from the city's best restaurant, he throws me a nod. Food delivery apps are my new best friend.

Once he leaves, I unpack. There's enough food here to feed an army, but it's just me. Spreading it all out on the kitchen island, it suddenly feels like a feast for one. A very lonely one.

I catch my reflection in the kitchen's chrome finish. My scruffy beard's grown longer, hair's a mess. Haven't had to worry about looking boardroom ready for a while. Honestly? I look like a rugged lumberjack who got lost and wandered into a billionaire's apartment.

Shaking off the thought, I focus on the meal before me. Steak, lobster, truffle fries, you name it. Eating is mechanical. I barely taste the flavors. It's rich and sumptuous but lacks the zest Violet brought to even the simplest dishes.

After eating, I aimlessly wander the apartment, eventually reaching the balcony. The night view is spectacular. Cars move like ants below, and the city's lights twinkle, reminding me of a distant galaxy.

But one thought intrudes, insistent as a throbbing ache: Away from Violet, this new universe is cold, empty. The dazzling lights below serve as a stark reminder of the singular, radiant star I've left behind.

I pinch the bridge of my nose, an attempt to shut out the swirling thoughts. She's getting hitched. To that tool. Of all people, seriously? Violet, with her mane of fiery red and those confounded freckles, in a white dress, walking towards... him. Jesus.

With fists clenched, I try to force the mental image out. What was it? A brief lapse of judgment, a mistake that I, of all people, got lost in her? With each heartstring she pulled, I fell. Like a rookie.

Then there's that gnawing question. The baby. Did she...? God, I can't even finish the thought. I never wanted to be 'that guy' but here we are, in the thick of a drama I'd rather switch off.

As for her parents, those two are chapters from a bad book I'd burn if I could. Puppet masters. I never understood how someone as bright and unique as Violet came from those two nitwits.

My folks? Well, they've never been fans of the "in-laws-to-never-be." In their defense, they've got a point. I mean, every family has its quirks, but Baileys? They take the trophy for dysfunction junction.

And just when I thought there couldn't be any more back-stabbing, enter Alec. Best friend? More like a backstabbing chum. Our past, all those memories, meant nothing when it came to choosing sides. Violet's bro traded our brotherhood for loyalty to his screw-up family.

I walk back inside, attempting to drown the anger with some good old whisky. The first sip burns, much like the memories. Violet and I, we had something. Now all I have are "what ifs" and a bitter taste on my tongue.

But you know what? If she's happy, if she's truly content, then so be it. I'll swallow this drink and these feelings. But it doesn't mean I have to like it.

Tapping my fingers on the bar counter, I admit to myself, maybe for the first time, how much I miss Alec. He was my brother in every sense but blood. But the way he sold us out, Violet and me? Alec invented one of those plot twists you never see coming. Damn, did it hurt.

Still, I'd like to escape all these stinging memories. This city, this apartment, they are cold solace. Here I am, a billionaire in a penthouse, yet feeling more caged than ever.

Maybe it's time for a change. I've started over before, right? Maybe I need a fresh start. Far from all this. Where no one knows my name, my story, my losses.

But for tonight, just one more drink. For the past, the love lost, the betrayals. And especially for those damn freckles. Cheers.

Each day blurs into the next. Swig of whiskey, swig of regret, and repeat. Honestly, it feels like a lifetime that I've been holed up in this luxurious prison.

The world outside keeps spinning. Violet's probably playing house, trying on white dresses, and tasting wedding cakes. I wish them joy. Or whatever the hell it is they're looking for.

Just as I'm perfecting my sour mood, there's a knock. My first thought? Who the hell has the gall to disturb me right now?

I pull open the door, half expecting some overly eager salesperson. Instead, it's Alec. Damn. I should've seen this coming. I told him where I was, just in case. You know, safety protocols.

I raise an eyebrow, the silent 'what the hell do you want?' He gets it. Always did.

Without another word, I turn and head back inside. There's a half-empty beer on the counter, and I grab it, letting the coolness settle in my hand. Cold beer, colder company.

Alec strolls in, uninvited but not unwelcome. The audacity of this guy. He takes a casual look around, as if he owns the place. Maybe he's sizing it up for a game of poker. I wouldn't put it past him.

"Well?" I prompt, taking a swig.

"Just checking on you."

I roll my eyes. "Lovely. Can I help with anything else, or are you here to gloat about the family reunion?"

Alec snorts, taking a seat like he belongs. Which, I guess he sort of does. After all, we've been through the wars together. But recent times? Not our best era.

I watch him for a moment. He's wearing that look. The one that says he's weighing his words. Considering. Calculating. Damn him.

He takes a deep breath, looking almost vulnerable. "I messed up, man. I know it."

I nearly spit out my beer. Honesty? From Alec?

"Not here for apologies," he grunts, but the edge in his voice isn't as sharp. Time does that, doesn't it? Sands the sharp edges into rounded corners and a soft ache.

I nod. "I didn't expect you were."

We sit in silence for a while, letting the weight of everything unsaid stretch between us. The room's filled with ghosts – past mistakes, regrets, and chances not taken.

Finally, he breaks the silence. "Vi's not…"

"Don't," I cut him off, feeling that familiar knot in my stomach. "I don't want to hear about her."

Alec raises an eyebrow but doesn't push. He's always been good at reading the room. Maybe that's why he's such a shark at poker.

"You staying?" I ask after another long pause.

He shrugs. "Only if you're sharing the beer."

I chuckle, despite everything. "One condition."

Alec arches an eyebrow, curious.

"No talking about… her."

"Deal."

The TV lights up with some B-list actors. They do their best to make a predictable script somewhat bearable. I mean, who chooses to rob a zoo for a rare bird? Only in Hollywood.

Alec lounges on the couch, getting comfy.

Still, there's a weird comfort in this. Two grown men watching a crap movie, side by side. Reminds me of the old days before everything became complicated.

"Nice place you got here," Alec remarks, glancing around. Sure, the penthouse is all sleek lines and modern luxury, but it feels…empty.

"It'll do," I grunt, sipping my beer. It's not home. But then again, where is?

"Missing the marble statues and gold faucets?"

"You know me," I shoot back, "Always fancied a good ol' golden toilet."

We chuckle, settling into an easy rhythm. Even with the distance between us, years of friendship can't be forgotten. Not over a couple of months of resentment.

Alec stretches, feigning interest in the movie. "So, you think they'll get the bird?"

I snort, "I'm more curious about how they're planning to fence it. It's not like you can just pop a rare parrot on eBay."

The room grows quieter than a church mouse's footsteps. The movie plays on. Its absurdity is growing even more poignant given the heaviness between us.

"Hey, um, I know you don't wanna talk about Vi but..."

I glance at Alec, one brow raised. His face, a mess of guilt and discomfort, practically screams Bad News Ahead.

"Spill it."

"She wanted me to... tell you."

Of course she did. Why confront me herself when she has a messenger?

"Tell me what?" I ask, though a sinking feeling in my gut suggests I already know the answer.

"That she's keeping the baby."

The taste of beer sours in my mouth, and the movie's antics fade into inconsequence.

"What?"

"Yeah..."

Images of Violet flood my mind. Violet pregnant. Violet holding a baby—our baby.

"What about... Cole?" The name tastes bitter on my tongue, the sting of betrayal fresh as ever.

"She's still marrying him."

I grit my teeth. Figures.

"And he's okay with that?"

Alec shrugs, looking anywhere but at me. "I don't know."

I snort. The thought of polished, perfect Cole playing step-daddy to my child? That's a sitcom I'd pay to see.

"That guy is a fucking clown."

Alec pauses for a moment, his face turning serious. "Speaking of Cole, I think I learned some stuff about him, but..."

I cut him off with a wave of my hand, not wanting to know. "I don't want to know. Focus on the wedding."

"And um... the wedding is... this Sunday."

Sunday? As in, five days from now? "That soon?"

Alec shifts uncomfortably in his seat. Then, like he's about to share a guilty secret, he leans closer. "Remember Alissa? Violet's best friend? She wanted your number, so I gave it to her."

I freeze, the beer bottle halfway to my lips. "What does she want from me?"

He glances around before dropping his voice to a conspiratorial whisper. "Well... she's talking about some... plan." Something about the intensity in Alec's voice and the serious look on his face catches my attention. I lean in closer.

"What plan?"

31

THE BRIDAL SHOP

VIOLET

My reflection stares back at me, drowning in layers of white and lace. Ugh, another one that feels like a marshmallow nightmare. I give my reflection a twirl, examining every angle. This one could use more sparkle, if you ask me.

"I like it," I chirp, giving a faux thumbs-up to the mirror.

Mama stands there, eyebrows shooting up to where her hairline used to be. "Vi, sweetie, you've said that about the last ten dresses!"

I shrug, feigning innocence. "What can I say? I have eclectic tastes."

She rolls her eyes, and I can almost see the smoke coming out of her ears. It's like witnessing the early stages of a volcano eruption. "We don't have all day. The shop closes in an hour."

I give her a mock salute. "Aye, aye captain! But you do realize this is the first time you've given me a choice in anything?"

Her eyes darken, and I can feel the storm brewing. "Violet, this is your day. I only want what's best for you."

I laugh, but there's no humor in it. "Is it? I feel like it's more for the society pages than for me. I feel like you're marrying me off, not like I'm choosing a partner."

Mama's face flushes. The shade matches the 'Hint of Blush' dresses she's chosen for the bridesmaids.

"You ungrateful little..."

"I'm not ungrateful." I interrupt, voice trembling, but stern. "I just want to have a say in my own life."

She stands rigid, every inch the matriarch. "I've always wanted what's best for you."

I laugh. It's bitter and dry. "Best for you and your reputation, you mean."

Her mouth pinches tight, fury evident. "At least we're letting you keep your...mistake."

My face goes cold. "You mean my baby? My 'bastard', as you so lovingly put it?"

She meets my gaze unflinchingly. "You know what I mean. This could've been a scandal. We're trying to maintain a certain image."

My eyes blaze. "Your image. Not mine. Not ever mine."

She throws up her hands, exasperated. "Fine! Choose whatever dress you want. Ruin the most important day of your life."

With a smirk, I retort, "Thanks. I think I will."

Our tension is like an overly frosted cake - sweet on the outside, but leaving a sour taste once consumed.

I pluck a random dress from the rack, not bothering to check its size or design. "This one." And without another word, I storm out of the shop.

I can hear the hurried click of her heels as she trails behind me. "Violet!"

Stopping abruptly, I turn around. "What?"

"Look, I'm sure you've seen the eviction notice as well."

"Yes," I snap, rolling my eyes. "It was pretty hard to miss."

"Listen, Vi... we need you to do this. Just... let him help us. After that, you can get a divorce, annulment, whatever you want. Just... see this through."

The bitter laugh that erupts from me is foreign even to my ears. "You never cared anyway, Mom. Why should I? Why would I help you and your husband's gambling addiction?"

Her face tightens. "That's your father you're talking about."

My eyes narrow. "What kind of father marries off his daughter? Was I another one of his lost bets?"

Her face turns an angry shade of crimson, but there's desperation in her eyes. I see the unspoken plea. But the weight of betrayal is too much, too fresh.

I slide into the once-pristine leather seat of our family's last-standing car. The scent of faded luxury wafting up to greet me. Of all the fancy rides we used to flaunt, this old beaut's the last one not snatched up by Dad's debts. Figures.

Mom makes a beeline for the passenger door. Part of me wants to gun it. Leave her flapping in the wind like those ridiculous feathery accessories of hers. But come on, even my patience has limits. And she is my mom, after all.

The engine purrs to life under my touch whispering, "Girl, let's escape." But where would we go?

Mom climbs in, smoothing her skirt and shooting me a look. That 'Mom-glare' – yeah, she's still got that.

So, we glide down the streets of our once-familiar neighborhood. Mansions, shrubs sculpted like animals I can't even name. And those ostentatious fountains everywhere. This whole place is one big, glorified peacock show. And soon, we won't even have a ticket to it.

Reaching our soon-to-be-ex-mansion, I can't help but muse. It's funny. The house looks the same, standing tall. Yet, everything inside its walls has crumbled. Maybe that's a metaphor for our lives or something deep like that.

Pulling into the driveway feels oddly final. It's amazing how a piece of paper stuck to your door can turn your entire life upside down. How did we even get here?

I rev the engine a tad too loudly as I pull into our driveway, but I make my stance clear. *No more Miss Pushover.*

My phone buzzes, but I ignore it for now. I'm headed straight for my room. My glittering heels click at a speed that would make an Olympic sprinter proud. But then the thought of Alissa, my best friend who's out of town, tugs at me, and I pause halfway up the grand staircase.

Fumbling for my phone, I shoot her a text.

I miss you. When will you be back?

I hit send, but guilt washes over me immediately. Am I being selfish? Her closest aunt from the east coast died and she has been with her family. I stare at the screen, my heart sinking, but there's no taking back the text now.

Shaking my head, I continue up the staircase, two steps at a time. Mom's hushed whispers and Dad's grumbling fade with each step. My room. Door slams behind me. Quick twist. Locked.

My head thuds against the door. One deep breath. Okay, maybe three.

Living with Cole? A guy whose personality resembles unflavored yogurt? Whose biggest achievement is successfully wearing socks that match? This should be interesting. But hey, life's tossed me some zesty lemons, might as well prepare for a sour ride.

But then I turn and...

32

REDISCOVERY

VIOLET

The sight of him hits me like a shot of tequila on an empty stomach. *Ryan*. Sitting there, on my flowery bedspread, looking all rugged. Not like a dude who just scaled a house.

Swallowing the shriek threatening to erupt, I force my words out in a fierce whisper. "What the actual fuck, Ryan?"

He gets up, all six feet 2 inches of his infuriating self, smirking. Oh, that smirk. One eyebrow raised, he says, "Thought I'd drop by, check on you. Oh, and the little munchkin too."

Shaking my head, I manage, "H-How the hell did you get in?! If my parents see you…"

"Your window was open. I needed a good workout."

"I thought you'd be out partying in some other state by now."

He doesn't even flinch, just gives me that intense stare. "Things changed when Alec mentioned… you know."

I sigh, letting the tension drain a bit. I sit next to him on the bed, creating an ocean of space between us. "I'm keeping our unexpected surprise."

"And playing happy family with Cole?" He side-eyes me.

His audacity. "Oh, come on! I'm not really over the moon about this arranged romance. Newsflash: wasn't my idea!"

Suddenly, his expression hardens, eyes darkening. It's like watching a storm brew in real-time. "Vi, that baby? It's half me. That is kind of a big deal."

Chewing on my lower lip, I glance at him, meeting the storm head-on. "You were clear about me keeping it."

His voice drops lower, rough like sandpaper. "I meant keep it with me. Our child shouldn't have to ask about its dad."

Short silence lets his words sink in and settle.

My hands clench into tight fists. Honestly, if looks could kill, Ryan would be six feet under by now. "Don't sound so shocked. Cole's a fixer-upper, I know, but desperate times, Ryan."

He stares, trying to process it. "So, it's just business? This isn't some twisted fairy tale?"

Rolling my eyes, I lean back, the cool wall pressing against my back. "I hate to break it to you, but I'm not Cinderella. The carriage is a pumpkin, and the prince is a debt collector."

"You're willing to trap yourself in a loveless marriage to save your family?"

And there it is, the million-dollar question. "Sometimes you gotta do what you gotta do."

Ryan's jaw clenches. He's pissed, I can tell. "So, you're going to play damsel in distress while your dad gets off the hook?"

I face him head-on. "Hey, I'm no damsel, alright? But family's family. As screwed up as mine might be."

"If you give a half a shit about me... Don't do this."

His voice, low and gravelly, pulls at something deep inside. It's like he's cracking open my vault of bottled-up feelings. Not fair, Ryan.

Before my brain can even register what's happening, there's this magnetic pull. The space between us? Vanishing. No more words. No more arguments.

Our lips crash together. Fireworks. Thunderstorms.

His grip tightens on my face, fingers tangling in my hair. Every ounce of restraint gone.

His other hand finds the small of my back, pulling me flush against him. Our breaths mix.

I bite his lower lip. He retaliates by nipping my neck. Goosebumps. Everywhere.

I pull back slightly, glancing towards the door. "Ryan... my parents are downstairs. If they knew you were here..."

His lips graze my ear. "They won't know." That voice, low and tempting, melts my resolve.

There's that audacity again. A whisper, a tug, and my jacket is on the floor.

The taste of him draws me back in. An impatient tug, a slide of fabric, and the room's temperature seems to skyrocket. Mom and Dad would have a field day if they walked in. But right now? I really don't give a damn.

He pushes me down and gets on top of me. I'm underneath Ryan, holding onto him as if letting go means losing everything.

A groan escapes him, and I can't help but smile. There's something about seeing Ryan like this, passionate and determined. His hands, rough yet gentle, know exactly where to touch.

"You look amazing like this, Vi,"

"Ryan," I breathe, unable to form anything more coherent. He smiles against my skin and continues his sweet torment.

Ryan's fingers find the hem of his shirt, and he pulls it over his head with a slow grace.

My heart somersaults in my chest. He's surprisingly gentle as he reaches for my shirt, his fingers tender and sure. Before I know it, my shirt and my bra join his clothes on the floor, and all that's left is the two of us, bared to each other.

Legs around his waist, I pull him closer. His cock is pressing against my pussy. His lips are back on me again, his teeth nipping at my lower lip, releasing only to dive back in.

And suddenly his boxers are gone, cast aside in a moment of need. My panties don't stand a chance either; he practically rips them from me. Yet through it all, his eyes never leave mine.

I lick my hand and reach to his hard throbbing cock while he is on top of me. I slowly start to stroke him with dexterity, making sure that every movement makes him want more.

Oh God. Me below him. Me here.

He starts kissing his way down, bringing my dream to life.

His lips find my inner thighs, kissing and teasing. Both my hands are in his hair, pushing him down, desperately trying to get more, but he doesn't yield. Oh, the way he teases my inner thighs, slowly making his way to my pussy.

He finds my clit, and a flash of knowing heat lights his eyes. Oh, is he good at that. Moving up and down real slow at first. Then he starts sucking on it like he's trying to tell me something without words. My pussy responds, getting wetter and more desperate with every flick of his tongue.

But soon I feel his fingers inside me, reaching deep. I find his tongue meeting mine again, and I can't stop moaning. I can taste myself on his tongue.

"Moan in my mouth while I finger you," Ryan growls into my mouth. My back bows, electrified, when he moves his sweaty slick hand down to grab my ass-cheek. Then all too soon he enters two fingers into me.

"Fuck, Ryan!" I yell as I bite down onto Ryan's bottom lip, making him smile against my panting mouth.

Ryan catching me off guard, pulling his fingers in and out, stretching me, testing me, but I let myself go, like I always do. I let the pleasure consume me and consume me it does.

I can't take it anymore; I need him inside of me. My legs wrap around his hips as he slowly pushes himself into me. The sensation is too much, too intense. "Ryan!" I moan, but he's quick to cover my mouth.

"Shh... Don't let them hear you," he warns.

But I can't control myself, I'm moaning, but he replaces his hand with his mouth. His hand finds my neck, wraps around it. God damn it! He chokes me slightly, just enough pressure to cut some blood circulation. A thrilling mixture of fear and pleasure races through me.

He then thrusts all the way in. His big cock is all the way inside me. How does something so wrong feel so right?

"Mmm... You feel so good, Violet," he moans into my mouth, his words vibrating against my lips.

His hand finds mine, fingers interlocking as if we're sealing a pact.

Then he picks up his pace. Faster, harder. My heart races to keep up.

He places both my legs on his shoulders, eyes locking with mine, as if asking for permission. Permission granted, darling.

The slow and sensual lovemaking soon becomes not enough. He's a man on a mission, practically bending me in half as he starts to move his hips faster.

The tip of his cock is hitting my cervix as he is pounding into me.

"R-Ryan, I'm gonna..." I gasp, teetering on the edge, eyes closing in bliss. I'm so close, maybe another push or two and I'd be there, but then he pulls out of me completely.

The shock and frustration are almost as intense as the pleasure was. I open my eyes to find him grinning, that wicked, knowing smile that says he's not done with me yet.

Oh, Ryan, you tease. But two can play at this game.

I turn him over, straddling him. I grab his throbbing dick, aligning the tip of it with my entrance. As I lower myself all the way down, I catch his eyes. He bites his lower lip, cheeks flushed with lust, and it's his turn to watch and want. And oh, he watches.

I move up and down slowly, savoring every inch of him. My moans grow a bit too loud, and he takes control, pushing me down from the back of my neck, capturing my lips. Now I'm moaning into his mouth, lost in sensation.

He must not like my slow rhythm, as his feet suddenly step hard on the bed, knees curling, and he thrusts up to meet me. That's when I lose it. "God, Ry, I'm gonna... I'm gonna..." He urges me on, "Come for me baby."

I can feel myself getting tighter around him, and that's when I find my release. I come hard and my tight walls help him finish inside me. My whole world is spinning.

I collapse onto him, both of us a breathless, sweaty mess. The world slows down again, and everything feels right. He leans in, his lips finding mine, and kisses me. In that moment, it's not just a physical connection; it's something more. Something that's ours alone.

I've missed him. I know it, he knows it, but now, lying here, it's something that needs to be said out loud. There, I say it. "I've missed you."

His eyes are soft, filled with the same emotion I'm feeling. He reaches up, his fingers gentle, and pushes a strand of my hair away from my face. I missed you too, he doesn't say, but I see it.

I roll off him, still tangled in the sheets and the intoxicating scent of us. His arm wraps around me, pulling me closer, and I can feel his heartbeat. It's calming, grounding, reminding me that this is real. It's not a dream; he's here with me.

Oh, damn, what now? My head's spinning as I lie here, still feeling Ryan's warmth around me, and the truth hits me like a freight train. I'm pregnant with Ryan's baby. I just had sex with him, and I have a wedding in two days. With Cole. God damn it.

I get up, wrapping a sheet around me, my mind racing. Cole's nice and all, but he's not Ryan. He's not the one who sets my soul on fire, makes me laugh, understands me like no other. And he's certainly not the father of my child.

I wander over to the window, staring out at the night, feeling lost. How did I end up here? When did everything become so complicated? The answer's simple, really. It's always been about Ryan, even when I tried to deny it.

I look down at my still-flat stomach, a hand instinctively going to where our child is growing. Our child. Ryan's and mine. It's real, and it's happening, and I have no idea what to do.

What now?

33

Soul Searching

RYAN

I'm sprawled out on Violet's bed, chest heaving. Man, it's been one wild ride, and I'm not just talking about the physical part. I glance at Violet, her cute, hooded eyes are sparkling.

Something in me snaps.

She can't be marrying some other guy. It's just wrong. Cole doesn't even know her like I do. He is just a placeholder. Me? I know the real Violet. And she knows me.

The way she moaned, the way her body responded to mine, that's not just lust. That's more. Way more. And now there's a baby on the way, my baby. And she is keeping it.

If Cole tries to lay a finger on her, he's dead. No, I'm not even kidding. It's a done deal. He's toast. I don't care what it takes; I'll protect what's mine.

I mean, what's the big deal about allowance anyway? Who cares about my parents' plan for my "perfect life"? That's not me. Not anymore. It's Violet I want; it's Violet I need.

I can hear the shower running. My mind's racing, and it won't slow down. Billionaire parents or not, there's something more valuable right here. And it's not the money.

I can almost hear my dad's voice, telling me to be reasonable. Think about my future. Put aside these foolish notions of love. But that's the thing, love isn't foolish. Not this time.

I glance at the closed bathroom door, wishing I could see her, touch her again. This isn't a game. It's real, and I can't turn away from it.

The water stops, and I hear the soft rustling of a towel. Violet's coming out, and I need to be ready. Ready to tell her my decision. Ready to assure her that it's her and only her.

My inheritance? Who needs it? My parents' approval? Not interested. All I care about is Violet and our future together. That's what's real.

The bathroom door opens, and she steps out, wearing shorts and a tank, her hair dripping wet. I look into her eyes, and I see it all. My past, my present, and my future.

And I'm ready. Ready to face whatever comes our way. Because she's worth it. She's everything.

"Hey," That's what she says, drying her hair with a towel, her smile not quite reaching her eyes. I get up, feeling a magnetic pull, brushing a strand of wet hair off her face. I'm about to lean in when she pushes me away, her eyes clouded with something unrecognizable.

What? What just happened?

"This -- This was a mistake, Ryan." Her words cut through me like a knife. A mistake? That's not possible. I can't breathe. I can't think. I don't understand.

I can see her face, her expression, the sadness in her eyes. And it doesn't make sense. Nothing makes sense.

"What do you mean, a mistake?"

"I-uh. I will be married soon, Ryan. And you know that. Why did you even come back? Why did you have to stir things up?!"

"You're carrying my child Violet!" The words are out of my mouth before I even know what I'm saying. But they're true. And they matter. They matter more than anything.

"That's it? You're only here because I'm pregnant?"

I pause for a second, thrown off by the question. But I know the answer. I've always known the answer. "No, Violet. You know that."

"Then why? Why did you have to come back and stir me up?!" She's yelling now, and her face is flushed, her eyes filled with tears. But I can't back down. Not now.

"Because… Because I love you, Violet."

Her face goes white, as if she's seen a ghost. She is looking at me like she doesn't know me at all. But she does. She knows me better than anyone.

"You love me?"

"Yes," I say, my voice firm. "I love you. And I want to be with you. I want to be with you and our child."

"But… But my parents…"

But her parents? Her parents can go to hell as far as I'm concerned.

"Your fucking parents again!" I'm yelling now, and she's shushing me.

"Lower your voice, they can hear you."

"Your fucking parents--" I almost whisper the words, but the rage is still there. "I'll talk to them."

"What? No. No, you can't do that, Ryan." She's panicked now, grabbing my arm, trying to stop me. But I won't be stopped. I can't be stopped.

"I can and I will."

"Ryan!"

She tries to stop me, holding my arm, but I turn back, cup her face, and say what needs to be said. "I'm not letting the woman I love get married to some scumbag because her father said so."

She is looking up at me with pleading eyes.

"I won't let them take you away from me, Vi."

Her eyes are filled with tears, but she doesn't say anything. Doesn't do anything.

"I'll talk to them," I insist, my voice firm. "I'll make them understand."

"You can't," she whispers, her voice breaking. "You can't change their minds."

"I have to try."

"They'll know you were up here. At least... at least talk to them later, Ryan."

"Fine." The word is short, clipped, but I soften as I brush her cheek with my hand.

I look at her, the fear in her eyes, the desperation, the love, and something in me snaps. I can't be gentle now; there's too much at stake. I pull her close, my hand firm against the small of her back. Our lips crash together in a kiss that's fierce and demanding.

34

Two Days

RYAN

She responds with equal intensity, her arms wrapping around my neck. Her body presses against mine. Our mouths explore and clash, teeth nipping, tongues tangling.

It's a kiss filled with all the frustration, fear, and longing that's been building between us. It's a kiss that says everything words can't.

I get behind her, kissing and biting on her neck. My hand leaves her body for a brief moment, leaving her skin feeling cold in the absence of my touch. After a second and a huff from her, I'm touching her again. All over, my hands trail from her shoulders to her chest, gripping and massaging in a way that makes her mewl.

I rub my cock against her ass, and she flinches unsuspectingly. She feels my lips on the back of her neck, sucking softly as I massage her ass with my right hand.

"Mm," I groan in her ear. She pushes her ass further against the bulge in my pants. My hand lands down on her ass with a loud clap in response, making her yelp and squirm.

"Can I take these off?" I ask, fingers already dipping past her waistband. She nods rapidly, barely sighing out a yes, I yank the shorts harshly down her legs, jolting her in the process.

I am in a dangerous position. The curve of her ass mesmerizes me, and I am so absorbed I almost forget that I am presently in this moment.

I swallow thickly, bringing my attention away from her backside and to her tank top. She has already begun to tug the hem upwards before I join her, pulling the top over her head in one smooth motion.

I push her gently to the bed. I remove all my clothes as she watches. I gently take her hand and place it on my dick. She slowly begins to rub it up and down as I slip two of my fingers inside her. "F-fuck, feels good," I moan as I notice her shiver slightly from the sensation. A soft blush spreads across her face.

Her pussy gets wet, and I know we're going to fuck soon. "Put it in me," she whispers as she uses her free hand to palm and finger herself. "I want you."

I groan and watch her touch herself for a moment before removing my hand from her warm, wet center. I settle my body on top of hers, wrapping my arms around her as I kiss her deeply.

"Not yet," I say after I touch my tongue to her bottom lip. I slowly grind my cock against her before making my way down her body. My lips leave a trail of soft kisses between her breasts and along her belly.

I gasp softly when I feel my tongue delicately run along her wet slit, tasting her. I tremble as I hook my arms around her thighs and begin to ravenously eat her inside and out. The way my mouth and tongue are working, you would think I've been starving for what she has to offer.

I hear her moan and feel her fingers thread through my hair. Her body starting to writhe as I pleasure her with my tongue. As usual, it's incredibly arousing, and I'm so lost in the sensation.

If I could just stay in this bedroom with my head between her thighs for the rest of my life, I'd be content. I'll never ask for anything else if I can give her orgasms on a regular basis.

"Fuck, you taste amazing." I announce after bringing her to the edge a few times.

"Don't stop," she moans, her need for release winding tight in her belly.

We both lock eyes. "Y-you're so beautiful, Violet, mhmm, fuck," I moan, and she giggles softly before closing her eyes. She smiles as she presses her fingers against my head, enjoying the sensation of my tongue inside her.

As I pick up the pace with my tongue she pleads, "F-fast, fuc-fuck faster, please." She gasps loudly, her cheeks flaring red. Her heart races as she tries desperately not to come yet.

"O-oh" she moans softly, arching her back slightly as her breathing speeds up. I lift my head as I withdraw my tongue, and I can see the frustration on her face.

"R-Ryan- p-please," she stammers.

"Please what?"

"Please fuck me."

"Good girl."

I think for a moment, "Here, move to the end of the bed, but have your legs hanging off of it, okay?" I say as I move up off the bed, now standing at the edge of the bed.

She hesitantly complies, getting onto the end of the bed, in the position I told her to be in. Her legs are hanging off the side of the bed, giving me a good view of her inner thighs.

I slowly insert my cock inside her, moaning a little. I begin to move in and out of her, my hands on the bed, using it as support.

"You feel- re-really good," she moans out as I slam in, and out of her as she crosses her legs around my waist.

"Th-that's right, take that cock. You're d-doing so good baby," I moan loudly, throwing my head back as my eyes roll to the back of my head.

Her body shudders as I slam into her, causing her to cry out. She grips the sheets tightly before moving her hands to my arms, her fingers digging into my skin. Her chest rising and falling rapidly.

"F-faster please Ryan!"

Gasping, going faster, slamming in, and out of her. The bed creaks under us both, the springs squeak as we make love. her boobs bounce wildly, sweat dripping down her face and hair.

She wraps her arms around me tightly, pulling me close to her as she cries out loudly. I pick her up, still slamming in, and out of her.

I begin to kiss her passionately, only breaking away for air. Then going back in for the kiss, moaning in her mouth as our tongues explored each other's mouths.

She begins to pant heavily, as her pussy tightens around my cock even more. Her juices flowing freely down between her legs. "Are y-you close baby?", I ask, moaning louder.

"Y-Yes...Y-Yes! It feels s-so g-good... Mmhm...," she pants. Her legs wrap around me tighter, holding me closer to her as her body quivers.

I speed up, "Fuck baby, close, so close, gonna, m'gonna come," I moan out, going faster.

"Ah yes!!!!" Violet yells as her body stiffens, and her hands squeeze my wrist hard. Then her hands grab my shoulders, gripping them tightly. Her chest rises and falls quickly, her heartbeat increases dramatically. Her breaths come in short, rapid bursts, and her body twitches violently.

"I'm so close," I moan out, louder now, not caring if anyone hears me. Violet's body shakes uncontrollably, and her eyes roll back into her head.

Her hands tighten their grasp on my shoulders, squeezing them painfully. Her legs clench together repeatedly, squeezing my waist, as she lets out a loud cry. Her entire body shaking, she's quickly reaching her climax.

That breaks me, and I spasm into orgasm, my body shuddering in time with my cock's throbbing release. I'm somewhat aware of Violet groaning my name and quickly pulling off of me so I can shoot my load on her belly.

Finished, I sigh and fall forward onto the bed beside her. Exhausted and still wracked with post-orgasmic spasms. I hear

Violet chuckle beside me as I clean my cum off of her belly with the sheet.

I then gently roll her to face me. She wraps her arms around me as I kiss her sweetly. Sometimes I think the intimacy of the afterglow is better than the sex. Right now though, everything is good.

Later, still intertwined with Violet in the soothing afterglow, a realization hits me. I speak up softly, "I should go soon."

Her eyes meet mine. We both know the reasons, and no words are needed to explain them further. I carefully disentangle myself from her warm embrace and begin to dress.

With a last lingering look, I open Violet's bedroom window, the same way I had come in. The world outside seems so different from the intimate haven we had created in her room. But reality calls, and it's time to answer.

"I'll see you soon," I whisper, pressing a final, tender kiss to her lips.

I then turn to the window, feeling her eyes on my back. I have to be careful. I have to be smart. But most of all, I have to be quick.

I glance out the window, scanning the grounds for any signs of movement. Any signs of security. But there's nothing.

I glance back at Violet, her face pale and her eyes wide. She looks scared. She looks lost. But I can't think about that now. I have to go.

I climb out the window, feeling the rough brick against my hands as I do. The drop is far, but I don't care.

I hit the ground with a thud, the grass soft and cool beneath my feet.

I have two days until her marriage to Cole. Two days to come up with a plan. Two days to save the woman I love. Two days to convince my billionaire parents to help the girl they don't approve of. The girl they think is beneath me. The girl I love.

I can't help but chuckle at the thought of kidnapping Cole. It's absurd but tempting. The guy's a prick and he's getting on my nerves.

But no, I need to be smart about this. I need to be careful. I need to find a way to make this right. For Vi. For our child

My mind races as I move along the dark streets. I need to talk to my parents and convince them to help. But how?

I reach my car, the sleek black metal glinting in the streetlight. I can feel the weight of the world on my shoulders as I slide into the driver's seat and drive off.

Making my way to our estate, I try to picture the scene ahead. My parents will be... thrilled to see me, especially after me spending the last couple of weeks out of town. Thrilled. Yeah, right.

As soon as I enter, I'm greeted by Mom. She hugs me, her arms warm and familiar, then breaks the hug and looks up at me, her eyes wide. "Oh Ryan!" she exclaims, and then she's hitting my chest, her voice rising. "Where the hell have you been?"

35

THE PLEA

RYAN

"Out of town," I'm trying not to let her see what I'm feeling, trying not to let her in. Not now. Not yet.

"Out of town? That's it?" she repeats, "Your dad is furious, Ryan. Were you with that girl Violet?" Her voice is accusing now, her eyes narrow, her mouth tight.

"Mom, calm down," I say, my voice steady, my hands on her shoulders. "I'll explain it all."

But she's not calming down. She's still going on, still accusing me, still pointing fingers. "That girl is trouble, Ryan! She's nothing but trouble!"

I can feel my blood boiling now, can feel the anger rising in my chest. "Mom, just stop!" I snap, my voice rising. "Just stop!"

"What's going on?" Dad's voice booms as he comes thundering down the stairs. I can hear the anger in his voice, can see the rage in his eyes. But I don't care.

"Hey, Dad," I say, my voice casual, my face a mask. Inside, I'm anything but calm.

Dad's face is red, his fists clenched. "Ryan? Where the hell have you been? I swear to God, I—"

"Bill, stop!" Mom's voice cuts through the room, sharp and cold. She's standing in front of Dad, her hands on her hips, her eyes flashing. "He's been out of town."

"With that Violet girl?" Dad's voice is a growl now, his face twisted with anger. He's losing control, and I can see it. I can feel it.

"No, Dad," I say, my voice steady, my eyes on his. "I just needed some time for myself."

"And you couldn't say so?" Dad's voice is rising now, his face getting redder. "We were going to call the police to get to you."

"They wouldn't do anything because you know I left voluntarily." I reply, keeping my voice calm, my face impassive. I make my way to the couch and sit down, my body relaxed, my mind anything but.

"Look, Dad... I need your help with something." This is it. This is the moment. Everything comes down to this.

"Oh, now you need help?" Dad's voice is a snarl, his face twisted with rage. He's losing control, and I can see it. I can feel it. But I won't back down. Not now. Not when there's so much at stake.

"Listen, Dad... Violet, she's carrying my child."

"I thought she was going to abort it. Isn't she marrying soon?" Dad's voice is cold, his eyes hard. He's not giving in. He's not backing down.

"She's marrying Cole. But she's keeping the baby." My voice is steady, my eyes on his.

"So that she could get money from you, huh?" Dad's voice is dripping with scorn, his face twisted with contempt. He's not listening.

"Dad, she's not like that." I need him to understand. I need him to see. I need him to believe.

"Her parents are, though. I bet that's why they let her keep it."

"Stop referring to my baby as 'it,' okay? That's your grandchild, whether you like it or not. Do you really want your first grandchild to be raised by a scumbag like Cole Harrison?"

Silence. The room is heavy with it.

"So, what do you want?" Dad's voice is flat, his arms crossed. He's challenging me, daring me. I know this game. I've played it before.

"They're forcing her to get married because they can't pay their debts.

"A classic. Poor girl, huh?" Dad's voice is a sneer, his face twisted with contempt. He's not taking this seriously.

"Dad... I love her, and I don't want her to get married to someone she doesn't love." My voice is quiet, my eyes pleading.

"We can't be dealing with Baileys, Ryan. You know about our past..." Dad's voice is a warning, his eyes hard. He's trying to stop me. He's trying to control me. Not this time, Dad.

"I don't care, Dad! What matters now is that I love her, and she's pregnant. I want you to support me through this one thing, please! Let me be happy, huh?" My voice is a shout, my eyes blazing.

Silence. Mom and Dad look at each other, their faces drawn, their eyes wide. They're lost. They're confused. They're scared.

Mom breaks the silence, her voice soft, her eyes on mine. "But her parents already made the decision. How would you even convince them?"

"I- I don't know. Not yet."

Mom's eyes are like daggers, and I can see Dad's face twitching, ready to explode. "Bill, can we talk for a second?"

They retreat to the kitchen, leaving me to stew in the living room.

I'm lost in thought, my mind a whirlwind. This is not how I planned to spend my evening. My phone vibrates, and I snatch it up, fingers tapping out a message to Alec.

Hey can we talk?
Whats up
How much do ur parents owe
Why you askin?

Just tell me
I dont know the exact number.
8 digits though.
Geez
Yeah
If I offered to pay them would your parents let Vi be?
We wont be needing that
What?
I'll explain later.
Just don't do something stupid alright?
I'll figure it out. I have a plan.

Ugh. You won't figure a shit out Alec. I toss my phone aside, a surge of frustration washing over me. Eight digits. That's a whole lot of zeros. Can I even do it? Is this what it's come to?

I glance at the kitchen, hear Mom and Dad whispering. They think they've got problems? They don't even know the half of it.

I pull myself off the couch and head to the bar, pouring a stiff drink. Dad's finest whiskey, because why the heck not? I knock it back, the liquid fire scorching my throat, the warmth spreading through my chest.

Just another day in the life of Ryan.

―ele―

RYAN

Here I am, standing at Violet's parents' door, heart pounding in my chest like a freaking drum solo. Deep breaths, Ryan. You got this. Knock, knock. Nothing. Dead silence. Come on, I don't have all day.

I ring the bell, then shift from foot to foot, the seconds ticking away like hours. Finally, the door creaks open, and there's

Mrs. Bailey, arms crossed, eyes narrowed to angry slits. "What the hell are you doing here? If you're here to see Violet—"

"I'm here to see you, actually, Mrs. Bailey. And your husband. May I come in?"

"We have nothing to discuss," she snaps, trying to close the door. But hey, I'm no pushover. I hold it, my face set, my voice firm.

"It's important. And you owe it to me. Your daughter is carrying my child."

She steps back, eyes wide, lips parted in shock. She motions me in, finally. *One hurdle down, about a million to go.*

The living room's neat and tidy, but who cares? Mr. Bailey's sitting there, glaring at me like I've just kicked his puppy. *Nice to see you too, sir.*

"So, what's this all about?"

"I want Violet to be free to make her own choices. And I'm willing to pay off your debts to make that happen."

Mrs. Bailey's lips curl into a sneer. "Trying to buy our daughter, are you? How generous."

"Call it what you want. I call it love."

"You think you can just come here and buy us off?" he roars. "You ruined my daughter's life, and now you want to throw money at us?"

I can feel the heat rising in my face, but I keep my voice steady. "Ruined her life? You're the one ruining it by forcing her to marry someone she doesn't love."

"Watch your mouth, boy!"

"You can't keep playing puppeteer with your daughter's life. It's not fair to Violet, and you know it," I shoot back, not backing down.

Mrs. Bailey jumps in, her voice cold as ice. "You should have thought about that before getting her pregnant."

"That's our business, not yours."

My voice is firm, my eyes locked on hers. "What I'm offering is a chance for her to live her life without your strings attached."

"You have some nerve coming here, offering money like it'll solve everything." Yeah, like Mr. Bailey's anger is solving anything.

"It won't solve everything," I admit, leaning back, my arms crossed. "But it's a start, and you know it. It will keep your daughter out of a loveless marriage."

The ball's in their court now. "You need to leave," Mr. Bailey finally says, his voice flat.

I stand up, my face set, my voice cold. "Then you're sentencing her to a life of misery. Hope you can sleep at night."

I turn and walk towards the door, every muscle in my body tense, my mind whirling. This isn't over. Not by a long shot.

I'm halfway to the door when Mr. Bailey hits me with that gem. "You'll pay child support anyway."

I stop dead in my tracks, turning around, one eyebrow raised. "Not unless the baby isn't mine."

His eyes widen, his mouth falls open. "What do you mean?"

"Isn't that what you plan to tell the world? That the baby is Cole Harrison's?" I can't help the smirk on my face.

Silence. It's like I sucked all the air out of the room.

"I'm not paying a dime unless you let me marry her," I finally say, breaking the silence.

"Marry her?" Mr. Bailey's voice is high-pitched, almost shrill. "She's marrying Cole Harrison, end of story."

"She's not marrying him, unless you want everyone to find out that I am the father of her baby." My threat hangs heavy in the air.

"You're bluffing," Mrs. Bailey says, her voice trembling.

"No, I am not." I lock eyes with Mr. Bailey. "Another scandal – think you can handle it?"

"Get out of my house now!" He's yelling, pointing fingers at me.

I raise my hands in surrender and leave, my heart pounding, my mind racing. It's impossible to convince them. Turns out we have to do this Alissa's way. Here comes Plan B.

36

TRUST IN THE NIGHT

VIOLET

Tomorrow is my wedding day. *Me, marrying Cole Harrison?* God, damn it. Never in my wildest dreams did I think this would be my life.

I only wanted to ride some waves, be a regular college student, and have fun. But here I am, marrying some guy I can't stand.

Yesterday, I overheard Ryan talking to my parents. Listening was like an out-of-body experience. I started to intervene, but something held me back. Ryan was saying everything that needed to be said.

I watched them from the corner of the stairs, heart pounding, knees weak. Ryan's voice was strong, determined, and filled with love for me. He was fighting for us. The realization brought tears to my eyes.

Now my room is filled with flowers and congratulatory cards. It's all a lie. I don't want any of it. I want Ryan, I want our baby, I want our life.

I text my best friend, Alissa, finally. She's been out of town for a funeral, and I've missed her like crazy. Having her here would've made everything so much easier.

My fingers tremble as I tap out a text to her, tears about to spill.

> ***Hey Alissa***
> Hey babe
> ***I'm struggling, Alissa.***
> ***My mind is so full.***
> ***I don't know what to do***
> Be back soon. Just hang on, alright?
> Wait for me. I'm hopping a flight today.
> I have a plan

My heart swells with gratitude for having her in my life. Alissa's more than a friend; she's a sister, a lifeline. Knowing she's coming back gives me strength. The mention of a plan, however, just makes me smile. Hair-brained scheme is more like it.

I put down the phone, a new resolve building within me. With Alissa by my side, and Ryan fighting for us, I feel like I can face anything.

The wedding's tomorrow, and my whole world is about to change. But no matter what happens, I'm not alone. And that's all I need to know.

Ryan... What are we going to do? I can't bring my thoughts together. Are we going to run away? Is he going to convince my parents? Or will he let me go through with this wedding?

What if I make a scene? I could call the police. I've always been the good girl. *Yes, Mom. Yes, Dad.* Always their precious little... puppet. Never disobedient, always playing my part.

But now I'm lost because all I knew in life was to listen to what they had to say. And now? Now I'm rebelling, and it's like learning to walk all over again.

When I look in the mirror, the girl staring back at me is both familiar and foreign. It's time to take control of my life, but how? Ryan and Alissa are my anchors, but ultimately, it's my life, my decision.

The answer doesn't come easily. Every option seems terrifying, every path fraught with uncertainty. But I know one thing for sure; I won't be a puppet anymore.

Tomorrow's the wedding. Tomorrow, I'll decide my future. And it's either going to be the beginning of a new life with Ryan or the end of life as I know it.

Night's come, and it's just me, my thoughts, and this little bump growing inside me. My phone's nowhere to be found, and I suddenly realize I don't have Ryan's new number. Typical. I pat my belly, promising the baby it'll all be fine, like I've got it all figured out. *Who am I kidding?*

I glance at the clock – midnight. Parents are off to dreamland, dreaming of money and social status, probably. Then a sound catches my ear. Startling but distantly familiar. I cross to my window and look out to see Ryan throwing rocks like a lovesick teenager from an 80s movie.

"Ryan?" I almost shout, then cover my mouth, giggling at the absurdity. He's there, grinning like an idiot, waving as if he's on a parade float. I motion for him to come up, rolling my eyes. Honestly, this man.

He's soon at my window. The window creaks open, and Ryan's face pops up, all sweaty and flushed from climbing. "I am getting better at climbing up here!" he exclaims, tripping over the sill and landing in a heap on the floor.

I can't help but laugh as he jumps up, posing like a victorious wrestler. "Ta-da!" he grins, and I shake my head, pulling him in for a hug.

"Nice entrance, Tarzan. Now, what the heck are you doing here?"

"Couldn't let you spend the night alone, Princess. Not with tomorrow looming over us."

I roll my eyes, but my heart swells a bit. "You really know how to pick your romantic moments."

"That's me, all heart and bad timing."

I sit down, biting my lip. "What if we run away? Elope? Start fresh? You know... Bonnie and Clyde?"

He takes my hand, squeezing it.

"As tempting as that sounds, they'd slap me with a 'kidnapper' label faster than you can say runaway bride. Let's hope Alissa's plan is smarter and safer than that."

How does he even know about her plan? Seriously? She hasn't even told me yet. Typical. I know I can't keep my mouth shut. All Alissa told me was the meeting place and the time.

I sigh, looking into his eyes. "Something smarter, something safer...something us? But what?"

"Something us? Well, that rules out anything normal or sane," he grins, and I can't help but laugh.

"Hey, normal is overrated. And who wants sanity?"

"True. A sane person wouldn't be climbing windows for you. And, hey, how is our beloved Cole doing?"

"I haven't heard from him in a while. I told him its bad luck to see or talk to the bride before the ceremony or whatever."

"Clever girl. Keep him away with superstitions. Always thinking ahead, aren't you?"

"Someone has to. If I left it to you, we'd be in Timbuktu by now."

"Timbuktu? Now that's an idea. Ever been?"

"You're not seriously considering it, are you?"

He grins. "Might not be a bad place to hide. Far from all this mess."

"We can't hide, Ryan. We have to face this, head-on."

He sighs, rubbing his temples. "You're right, of course. But a guy can dream, can't he?"

"Dreaming's fine. Just don't pack your bags for Africa yet."

"No? What about... Tahiti? I hear it's a magical place."

"Only in the movies. Focus, Ryan. What's our real plan here?"

"Real plan? Haven't had one of those in years."

"You're hilarious. Now help me figure this out. We're in this together, remember?"

"Right, right. Together. Just like old times, but with more at stake."

"That's the spirit! But seriously, what's the plan?"

He frowns, thinking. "Let's make a deal with your parents. Offer them something they can't refuse."

"Like what? We've got a baby, not a mafia empire."

"What about convincing them this wedding is a disaster for the family image? It's not like you love the guy."

I tap my chin, pondering his words. "You might be onto something. Maybe we leak the truth, let it slip that I'm being forced?"

"You think they'd back down?"

"They have to protect their reputation. It's their Achilles heel."

His eyes light up. "Then let's hit them where it hurts."

I smirk, feeling the thrill of rebellion. "Who knew we'd turn into mastermind schemers?"

He raises an eyebrow, his voice dripping with mock seriousness. "I've always known you were a bad influence."

I feign a gasp. "Me, a bad influence? I'll have you know, mister, I was an exemplary child before you came along.

"Exemplary? Look at us now, plotting away. You sure you're not secretly related to Machiavelli?"

I laugh, grabbing a pillow and playfully hitting him. "Keep talking, and you'll be sneaking out that window sooner than planned."

I lay on my bed, and he lays next to me. We are both staring at the blank ceiling.

I rest my head on his chest, feeling his heartbeat. "You know, I've had a crush on you since high school." It's like a confession that's been trapped inside me forever.

He laughs, stroking my hair. "I've never had the luxury of loving someone before."

"Parents really get to you, huh?" I murmur, feeling a bit like a rebel teenager again.

"Yeah, parents suck." His chest rumbles with a chuckle. "I feel like a rebel teenager all over again."

"Me too." The thought makes me smile.

"So, when will Alissa arrive?"

"Her plane probably already landed." I pause for a second. "She loved her aunt. It was a shock to her, so I don't blame her for leaving."

There is a short silence before I add, "Everybody has their own problems."

I feel his arm tighten around me. "We will have our own little problem soon." I can hear the grin in his voice.

I chuckle, knowing he's talking about the baby. "I hope it's a girl."

"A girl?" He seems intrigued. "Why?"

"Yeah." I look up at him. "I'd like to raise a girl who doesn't have to worry about the things that I did. A girl who isn't protected from life, who doesn't have traditions and appearances pushed down her throat."

He kisses my head, and I feel warm and safe. "That sounds perfect."

I look at the time on my phone. It's almost time to sneak out and meet Alissa.

But I have never snuck out before.

"Seriously, never snuck out before?" He's trying not to laugh, I can tell.

"I've always been a good girl, I guess." I shrug, trying not to look as clueless as I feel. My phone buzzes in my hand - a text from Alissa.

Almost there.

Ryan reaches through the window, taking my hand. I hesitate for just a moment, then let him guide me out, clumsy and unbalanced.

He steadies me, his touch gentle. "Don't worry, I've got you."

I can't help but laugh at myself. This good-girl-gone-bad act is harder than it looks.

We make our way to the car, and I can feel the excitement bubbling inside me. Alissa's plan is on.

Ryan and I make our way to the meeting spot in a private garden near Alissa's home. The owners are abroad for the summer. Streetlights flicker as we approach the shadowy figure in the distance. It's Alissa, my rock, my confidante. My heart races. It's been too long.

We reach her, and without a word, she pulls me into a tight hug. I feel the warmth, the connection, and a tear threatens to escape. She almost cries too. Ryan looks on, a knowing grin on his face. Something's up.

I pull away, eyes wide. "Guys... what the hell is going on?"

Alissa smirks. "We talked about it."

"But how?! When? He has a new phone and everyth--"

"Alec."

"What?"

"He helped."

My jaw drops. "Why didn't you tell me?"

"You're a bad liar, Violet. We didn't want any slip ups to tip off your parents. Or Cole."

I pout but can't argue. "Well... fair enough, but... what's the plan?"

Ryan and Alissa look at each other, eyes gleaming with excitement and determination. It's happening. The wheels are in motion, and our lives are about to change.

37

THE LAST GAMBLE

RYAN

So, here we are, the three of us, all set to tackle whatever Alissa's cooked up. But then there's a noise, a rustling, and Violet's eyes go wide.

"Speak of the devil," she murmurs, and I turn to see what she's staring at.

Alec, walking up like he owns the place, wearing that cocky grin, although his eyes are a little unsure.

"Hey, Sis," he says, addressing Violet, but she's not looking too pleased.

My eyes are on Violet, and I watch her face pass through an ocean of surprise, anger, hurt, and then something softer. It's a mash up of feelings, and I'm staying out of it. I do slip my arm around her waist for support.

Alec looks at me, and I give him a nod, my way of saying, *'You handle this, buddy.'*

He steps closer to Violet, his face serious now. "I want to help. I'm here for you."

Her eyes fill with tears, but she's holding them back. Tough girl. Finally, she whispers, "I certainly hope that's true."

He nods, and the tension drops a notch.

"I have evidence," Alec finally speaks, explaining how he managed to get what we needed. His manner is like the old Alec of our early friendship, the man with the plan.

"First, we need to expose Cole's sketchy business dealings," Alissa begins.

"How?" Vi interjects, but Alissa's not thrown off.

She continues to explain that Alec has managed to hack into Cole's secret accounts. He discovered numerous shady transactions. She's confident, and I like it.

"We will expose the shady Cole to the public, let everyone see who he really is. Newspapers, social media, the whole shebang."

I can tell Vi's still trying to catch up, but that's why we are here.

"But what about the money?" Vi asks, frowning.

Alissa is ready for that question. "We'll use Cole's own greed against him. We'll lure him into a trap, make him think he's investing in something foolproof. But in reality, he'll be paying off your parents' debt."

I see the confusion in Vi's eyes. Cute, but we need her on board.

"Think of it as a phantom investment, a mirage. He'll see what he wants to see, but in the end, the money will be rerouted to your parents. Legally grey but effective."

I can see Vi's starting to get it now. She's nodding, asking questions, really getting into the details.

"We've got everything set up," Alissa reassures her. "The accounts, the paper trail, all leading back to him."

Vi's still asking questions. But I can see her confidence growing, and it's giving me butterflies. There's that sparkle in her eyes. She's not just following along; she's part of the plan.

"This will work," Alissa assures us, and I believe her.

We're all in agreement.

We're ready to put the plan into motion, and everyone is on their toes, phones ready, documents in hand.

I glance at Violet, our eyes meet, and we both nod. Game face on.

Alissa makes the first call.

"So, here's how we lure Cole," Alissa says, the scheming genius. "We make him believe that if he doesn't pay, he's ruined."

Vi's listening, her eyes sharp. "But what if he doesn't buy it?"

"That's where the evidence Alec put together comes in," Alissa smirks. "We show him a taste, just enough to scare him."

Alec is showing us one page of Cole's hacked bank account. All of Cole's pay offs, bribes and hush money paid to politicians and CEOs. There are some sketchy figures in black and white. Plus, the corresponding deposits from innocent and unsuspecting victims resulting from the pay offs. It's perfect.

"Now we call him," Alissa says, taking out a newly purchased, totally untraceable cell phone. "Anonymously, of course."

We listen on speaker as she dials, the tension thick. Cole answers, his voice sounding unbothered as he answers. "Cole Harrison."

"You've been a naughty boy, Cole," Alissa's voice is all threat and ice.

"Excuse me?" he snaps.

"You should have been more careful," she continues, and I can hear the uncertainty in Cole's voice.

"Who is this?" he demands.

"The person who knows everything," Alissa replies. "The person with records of your payoffs. And corresponding deposits from innocent victims who trusted you and your henchmen."

"That's preposterous and impossible. I have no idea what you are talking about." Cole's voice cracks.

"Oh, but I have evidence, and I am prepared to expose you. Check your inbox for a preview of what will be sent to all major news outlets and posted to social media. It will happen in one hour unless you follow my instructions immediately."

There's silence, presumably as he checks his email. Then Cole's voice, edged with panic, returns. "And just what instructions are those?" Cole's voice is slow and deliberate. .

"Ten million dollars," Alissa says without hesitation. "To the bank account I just texted to you."

"But that's not--"

"Do it, or your reputation is ruined. And just remember. It isn't your reputation alone that is on the line. This includes the reputation of your bribed associates, on both sides of the law."

Alissa cuts in. "You have one hour to check the authenticity of the documents and make your decision."

She hangs up, and we all let out the breaths we have been holding.

"Do you think he will really do it?" Vi asks, her voice tight.

"He has no choice. Some of his so-called associates can do more harm than ruin his reputation." Alissa answers, confident as ever.

Alec is monitoring the account on his phone, ready to verify that the money has been received.

We wait, the minutes dragging on, hearts pounding. The stakes are high, but we're higher.

I hold Violet's hand, squeezing my support.

Then Alec's voice, triumphant. "He did it! The money's transferred."

We're cheering, hugging, jumping up and down in celebration. We pulled it off.

But this isn't the end. Not yet. We have more to do, more to win.

We're on the path, though, and the future looks bright.

Who would have known this guy would have such illegal stuff going on? I never liked him, but bribery, illegal payoffs, theft? Probably why Mr. Bailey lost so much money to him in the first place.

"Is this... legal?" Vi asks, her eyes wide.

"He can't go to the police," Alec says, smirking. "After these posts, he would be arrested or in fear of his life from his burned associates."

"Why didn't you tell our parents?" Vi asks, her voice rising.

"They wouldn't have believed me," Alec shrugs "Cole stood too tall in their minds."

"Why didn't you tell me?" Vi's almost pleading now.

"I've been trying to get close to him," Alec explains. "I knew something was off, Vi. I had to do some... research."

"You call this some research?" Alissa interjects, eyeing the evidence.

"I know, I know, I'm a genius," Alec grins, unapologetic.

"Hey, don't brag too much now, Alec," Alissa chides. "We have a couple to send to Brazil."

"What?" Vi exclaims, turning to me.

I can't help but smirk. I knew this part of the plan all along.

Vi looks at me, her eyes wide, searching. "R-Ryan?"

"We're leaving now, Violet," I say, my voice firm, full of promise.

VIOLET

Brazil! Ryan planned this escape, and I'm still trying to catch up. The grin on his face, the spark in his eye – I can't help but shove him lightly. "You sneaky little..."

"I'll miss you," Alissa chokes out, her eyes glistening.

I pull her into a tight hug. "We'll be back, though, right? After things settle?"

"How about passports and everything?" I ask, my mind racing.

"All handled," Alissa says, smiling at Alec. That brother of mine, I swear.

"You guys are... sneaky." I hold Ryan's hand, squeezing tight. We've done it. We've actually done it.

"Shall we?" Ryan asks, his eyes full of promise.

"Yes."

"Oh Sis, before you go..." Alec starts, and I turn to him. He's got that soft look in his eyes. Oh boy, here come the waterworks.

"Come here." He hugs me tight.

I bury my face in his shoulder, breathing in the scent of home. Then I hug Alissa, her body shaking with silent sobs.

"We'll be back soon," Ryan says, his voice gentle. "Just make sure to get your parents used to the idea."

"Man, you've given me the hardest task," Alec mumbles.

Alissa snorts. "Yeah, like teaching a cat to play fetch."

They all laugh, and I join in, the sound bubbling up from deep inside.

We say our goodbyes, and the car door slams shut. Ryan starts the engine, and I glance back, watching my family grow smaller in the rearview mirror.

"Ready?" Ryan asks, his voice soft.

"Ready," I whisper.

And we drive. We drive away from the lies, the hurt, the betrayal. We drive toward a new beginning, a fresh start, a future filled with love and laughter and possibility.

The road stretches before us, and I can't help but smile. The adventure is just beginning, and I have the best partner in crime a girl could ask for by my side.

Oh, life. You sure know how to keep a girl on her toes. Ryan has that mischievous grin on his face again. It's contagious. I find myself smiling too.

"Wait, are there big waves in Brazil?" I ask, my voice rising with excitement.

"Big waves? Baby, they've got the best surf spots in the world. We're gonna have a blast."

I giggle. "A surf baby! Can you imagine? Tiny surfboard and all."

He winks at me. "We'll raise the coolest surf baby in the world. No doubt about it."

The car glides through the night, but the world outside doesn't matter. It's just us, laughing and dreaming, plotting our grand future.

I poke him playfully. "We need to plan, you know? Surf spots, baby names, a new life."

He grabs my hand, kissing the knuckles. "We've got all the time in the world. No rush, no pressure. Just us."

A sudden thought hits me. "Oh my gosh, baby surf diapers! How cute would that be?"

He chuckles. "You're one step ahead. As always."

The road ahead is wide open, just like our future. We have the chance to write our own story, create our own destiny.

Ryan squeezes my hand. "What do you think? Surf championships for our baby? Or maybe, just enjoying the waves, taking life as it comes?"

I rest my head on his shoulder and then pull back, narrowing my eyes at him. "Wait a minute, you're not planning to make our kid do those crazy 360 spins on the waves, are you?"

He laughs, looking almost guilty. "Well, it crossed my mind."

I give him a mock glare. "Over my dead body! Our baby's not going to be some surf stunt double. I mean, maybe just a bit..."

He grins. "See? You're coming around. How about a surf detective? Solving wave-related mysteries."

I snort. "A surf detective? That's the most ridiculous thing I've ever heard. But it's strangely appealing."

He nudges me. "That's why you love me."

I roll my eyes but can't hide my smile. "I love you despite your crazy ideas."

He pretends to be hurt. "Ouch, that stings. But you know what? You're stuck with me."

I laugh, feeling lighter than I've felt in ages. "Stuck with you, huh? I guess I can live with that."

We drive in comfortable silence for a while, each lost in thoughts of our new adventure. Waves, surf detectives, life in Brazil – it's all just a bit insane. But then again, so are we.

38

EPILOGUE

VIOLET
Six months later

"The pictures didn't do you justice! You are glowing," Alissa squeals as she hugs me and rubs my belly, which feels more like a barrel these days. My friend is as gorgeous as ever, slender and tan in a yellow pantsuit.

"Really? I feel like a piñata." I laugh, adjusting my flowing hibiscus-flowered dress. "I missed you soooo much!"

Alec is hanging back, chatting with Ryan about the flight delays, waiting for his turn to greet me. "Hi, Sis, you look great," he says, somewhat shyly, giving me a side hug.

"How was your flight? Anyone hungry, besides my wife, that is?" Ryan offers with a chuckle. "Want to grab some food before we head to the hacienda?"

"Of course, we need to eat, but first, I need a restroom. Come on, Lissa," I say grabbing my friend by the hand. "You guys find the luggage and we'll meet by the entrance."

In the restroom, I catch Lissa's reflection in the mirror. I realize she is grinning way too much for someone who just stepped off a long plane ride. "Ok, spill it. What's putting that sheepish grin on your face? Or should I say who?"

She hesitates, rolls her eyes upward, before answering. "Well, Alec has been staying with me in Torrance, and..."

"My brother? Get out. You two together?" Surprise and excitement flood through me, but mostly surprise.

"Whoa, it's very new, I'm not sure where it's headed. It just sort of happened as we were planning our trip down here. We were talking, texting, and then he just sort of showed up this week," she explained. "I'm not sure what's going on, but I like it. And I think he does too. He's really changed, loosened up since you've been gone."

I shake my head. "Surprised, not surprised, I guess. But anything that has you glowing and grinning from ear to ear must be a good thing. Just don't call me Sis."

"Don't get ahead of the game. We haven't had much chance to see where it goes, but at the very least it will make for a nice vacation, so let's just see. And please, please, please don't say anything to Alec before I know more," she pleads.

I make the age-old motion of locking my lips and hug her to seal the deal. "I won't mention it again. Now let's go eat. I'm starving," I say as I head for the door.

I follow Alissa as she pushes open the door just as I feel a long hard kick and pain shoots through my lower back. I bite my lower lip. *Okay, little one, we'll be home lying down soon enough. Hang in there.*

RYAN

"The doctor says any day now, so we are on high baby alert," Ryan says as he pours wine for Alissa and Alec. "So water only for Mama and Papa to be. The baby go bag is in the back of the Land Rover and a nurse is standing by at home, just in case."

Alissa's eyes go wide. "You aren't having a home birth, are you?"

Violet laughs so hard water spurts out of her mouth. "Heavens, no. Get me to the hospital and get me the drugs as soon as possible! Rosita is there just to help me, advise me if labor starts. And she'll be our nurse and nanny when we leave the hospital."

"Our place is an hour from the hospital," I explain, "and she's coaching us both on childbirth breathing and massage. Vi walks a mile twice a day and is exercising, getting ready to bring our baby girl into the world." I cover Vi's hand with mine and squeeze it with pride. "She is gonna be the best mother."

"I may not look it, but I'm really fit and ready for labor," Vi offers, in a cheerful voice. But I see her bite her lower lip. My heart fills with love and I raise her hand to my lips.

Conversation continues about Alissa's school year and Alec's latest enterprises. I am content to listen, but I can't keep my eyes off Vi, who is showing some signs of being tired. Her shoulders are a little too tall, squared back and she is rubbing her lower back a little more than usual. *I need to get her home and put her to bed. It's been a long day.*

I motion to the waiter for our check.

VIOLET

Ok, you have my attention now, my precious. We aren't waiting until morning, are we?

Ryan's breaths are deep and even beside me and I take a few minutes to breathe in the sight of him. *This is the last time it will be just the two of us.* My heart skips a little at the thought that this is really happening.

Watching Ryan sleep is still my most treasured time. His blonde hair, strong arms folded on his chest, lips slightly open. Those visions all combine to fill me with a happiness and peace I never dreamed possible. Of all the pleasures and changes the two of us have experienced in the past months, lying here beside him tops them all.

"Hey, Lifeguard. I need you," I whisper. "Our baby girl is ready."

Ryan's eyes are open and alert in an instant. "Are you okay, Vi?" he whispers as he reaches for me.

"Yes, we are both fine, but we need to get going." I smile. Ryan is in motion, taking control. He helps me dress, bending to put sandals on my feet while murmuring words of encouragement and love.

"I'll let Rosita know and she can tell Alec and Alissa when they wake up. They can drive the Jeep to the hospital in the morning. We're ready, baby, let's do this."

Ryan is holding my hand with one arm supporting my waist as we step into the moonlit night. Guiding me, holding me, telling me to be careful, telling me he loves me, reassuring me.

I take a moment to look to the sky and the infinite stars shining just for me. This is what love looks like. This is what love feels like.

RYAN

Violet is sleeping, her hair still damp from labor, her bare shoulders above the white sheet. But a look of contentment and a slight smile rest on her lips.

I have one eye on her, but my arms are filled with my new daughter. Her small pink hat frames her still rosy skin, wrapped in the warm hospital blanket. *I want to hold you forever, little girl. How will I ever be able to lay you down in the bassinet rolled beside your mother's hospital bed?*

As if from nowhere, Alissa and Alec appear. They're standing before me holding a vase of pink roses and a heart-shaped helium balloon.

"I didn't hear you come in. I'm too engrossed in this little wonder," I explain, moving slightly to show off my girl.

The two of them ooh and aah, but I make no move to share her with the visitors.

When Lissa asks her name, I explain that I promised Vi I would wait to share the details.

"I will say Violet was a champ. She would win hands down if there were a competition for having a baby. According to her doctor, labor was quick and as easy as possible due to her being fit."

"And I had a good coach," Vi adds from her hospital bed.

I move to the bed to kiss her and lay the baby in her arms to let her make the introductions, kissing them both on the forehead.

"Alec, Alissa, meet Iris Victoria Ryder, 7 lbs. 2 oz. 19 inches long," Vi announces.

I watch as Alec and Alissa hug my family and present their gifts.

"Iris means rainbow, for all the colors including Violet. Victoria is for the victory we have both won in our new life together," I explain proudly.

"The new Ryder generation, Brazilian branch," Violet exclaims.

"Congratulations!" Alissa and Alec say in unison as they hug me from each side.

And I know my true life is just beginning.

The End

Thank you for reading *A Baby with my Billionaire Surfer*

If you loved this book, you will love ***Billionaire Protector***

Turn the page for the book synopsis

My billionaire boss can't take his naughty eyes off me...and I like it.

He's sexy – He's Romeo, Adonis, and James Bond all rolled into one.

Max is off-limits though...he *is* my boss after all.

Turns out he's more than just that – Max is my protector, my defender.

He steps in to shield me when my psycho ex comes back and threatens me and my daughter.

Sparks are starting to fly, and when he stands up for us, the fireworks of passion can't be denied...or contained.

Especially when he finds out my daughter is sick and he's the only one that can help her.

Scan to get *Billionaire Protector*

Here's a Sneak Peek from Chapter 1:

OLIVIA

My quest is interrupted by the jolt of colliding directly with another person. Both of us jump, the two cups fly from my grasp, and the warm coffee splatters across the lapel and pocket of an expensive burgundy suit.

"Oh, my goodness, I'm so, so sorry!" I apologize frantically, my words tumbling out automatically.

I swiftly dispose of the coffee cups in a nearby bin, carefully placing my other items on the floor, and begin to rummage through my bag for wipes to salvage the stained fabric.

As I dab at the stains on the suit in true mommy mode, I notice the fabric I'm attacking. *Damn, this looks like the same suit that Akizo Romani wore on the Runway last night. It must be incredibly expensive.*

I raise my eyes and meet the green-eyed gaze of the man wearing the exquisite suit. Time seems to stand still as an unexpected wave of attraction and distant familiarity washes over me.

"You're..." I stutter, my voice catching in my throat.

But before I finish my sentence, I notice his piercing glare, his expression filled with annoyance. Panic floods through me, and I begin to beg forgiveness.

"Oh my god... you're... you're him..." I whisper, my voice barely audible as the realization hits home. *He's Max Cooper, the CEO of the company.*

His eyes soften, and he extends a hand towards me. "Yes, I believe I am. And you are?"

"Olivia Hernandez," I answer, my voice hoarse with nervousness. "I'm Olivia." I manage to say again, my voice stronger this time.

"I am truly sorry for the coffee mishap. I promise this won't happen again. I got distracted and –" He cuts me off with a wave of his hand.

"It's all right, Olivia. These things happen. Let's not dwell on it. Now if you'll excuse me, I have a meeting to attend."

My mouth is still open as I watch him walk toward the elevator, disappearing into a group of other executives.

I had no idea how totally handsome Mr. Cooper is. Yes, I've seen photographs, but they definitely don't tell the whole story.

Broad shoulders, buff chest, rugged jawline, and perfectly symmetrical face with those piercing green eyes. Other than his sexy temples of gray hair, you'd think he was in his early thirties, but gossip columns report mid-forties.

Damn! I've never been this close to such a hunk of man.

This age-gap workplace romance is a stand-alone novella. There are extra-steamy scenes and rough language, but no violence, rape, incest, or menage. **And Happily Ever After ending, of course!**

Scan to get Billionaire Protector NOW!

Printed in Great Britain
by Amazon